THE GOOD-LUCK BOGIE HAT

By the same author

Leo the Lioness
A Girl Called Al

CONSTANCE C. GREENE

THE GOOD-LUCK BOGIE HAT

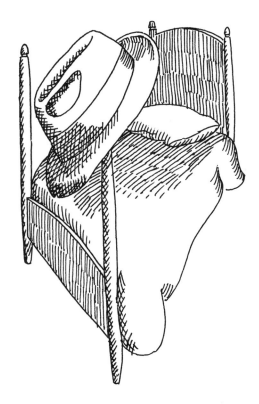

The Viking Press   New York

For Phil, with love

How do you like them apples?" Ben asked. "Look at the kid. Sharp. I mean really sharp. Beautiful, baby. Just plain beautiful."

He threw back his head, making slits of his eyes while he admired his new vest in the mirror. It was bright red with brass buttons and practically no moth holes.

His brother Charlie sat on the edge of the bed and watched Ben get dressed. He put his clothes on in layers. For underwear he wore cut-off jeans and a Camp Okachobee T-shirt. He had been a counselor-in-training last summer at Camp Okachobee.

"I know plenty of guys who don't wear any underwear at all," Ben said.

"Where'd you get the vest?" Charlie asked.

"Sammy's. Where else?"

Ever since Ben had discovered Sammy's shop in an

alley behind the railroad station he had been a cool dresser. Sammy dealt in old clothes and the price was right. He bought up whole attics and closets full of stuff when people moved or did their spring cleaning.

"Take me with you next time you go to Sammy's?" Charlie asked.

"Sure." Ben patted his vest fondly. "I know a guy who wrote an essay on why he didn't wear any underwear and the teacher gave him an Incomplete and said he'd have to write another paper if he wanted to get credit for the course. Some people have no sense of humor."

"Why didn't the guy wear any underwear?" Charlie wanted to know.

"He said he was so secure he didn't have to," Ben explained.

"You forgot your pants," Charlie said.

"Hey, comrade, you're not going out like that, are you?" Ack Ack Ackerman, a friend of Ben's, put his head around the door jamb. "The fuzz'll throw you in the pokey. They'll also throw the book at you if you go down Main Street with those gorgeous gams exposed."

A lot of people, mostly parents, thought Ack Ack was sort of peculiar looking. He was very tall and thin and kept looking over his shoulder as if he were being trailed. Charlie always knew when it was Ack Ack on the telephone. "Ben there?" his voice, low and whispery and quick, would ask. You couldn't be too careful. There might be a wire tap on the phone. Even when he was calling home to say he'd be late or could he stay for dinner at a friend's, he talked the same way. He'd put his hand over the receiver and turn his head rapidly from left to right to make sure no one was listening. Actually, it was Ack Ack's ambition to be on the Ten-Most-Wanted-Criminals list. "That's class," he said. "Only ten cats they want and you're one of them. I mean, how exclusive can you get?"

Of all of Ben's friends, Ack Ack was Charlie's favorite. Mostly because he treated him like an equal, not like a kid brother.

"Peace." Ack Ack lay on the floor and put his feet on Ben's record player.

"I didn't believe you when you said you were fifteen pounds underweight for your height, comrade, but now I get a load of your pins, I do believe," Ack Ack said.

Ben looked at his legs. They *were* skinny.

"But look at those calves," he said. "It isn't often that you see such a well-shaped calf."

"Only down on the farm," Ack Ack said.

Ben fished a pair of denim work pants out from under the bed and put them on. Then he donned a pair of scruffy desert boots he'd bought off a kid at school for ten cents. He was set.

"How much did the vest set you back?" Charlie asked.

"Seventy-five cents. For anyone else it'd be a buck. For me, seventy-five cents. Plus a shirt thrown in for good measure. Sammy and I have rapport," Ben said, smiling.

Charlie didn't know what *rapport* was but he wished he too had it with Sammy. Charlie had never met him but he figured he was a good man to know.

"You better get out before Mom sees you, Ben," Charlie advised. "You know how she is."

Ben gave a final check to his outfit. He wore a brown-and-blue striped shirt under the red vest and a Brooks Brothers sport jacket whose shoulder seams came halfway to his elbows.

"If they had a list of best-dressed citizens in this town, you'd be on it," Ack Ack said solemnly.

"Funny thing," Ben said, pleased. "I mean, I used to not care what I wore. I'd wake up in the morning and put on any old thing that happened to be lying around. I couldn't care less. I never thought I'd turn out to be a sharp dresser. The same thing will probably happen to Charlie when he's my age."

"I doubt it," Charlie said. "I only like hats. I'd sure like to have that black hat of yours. You hardly ever wear it. Why not give it to me?"

"Not my good-luck Bogie hat," Ben said, taking the black fedora from the bedpost where it had been hanging for weeks. It had a huge floppy brim, and when Ben put it on and pulled the brim down over his eyes and talked out of the corner of his mouth, he really did sound like Humphrey Bogart.

"Not this hat. This is one in a million. When they made this baby, they threw away the mold." Ben put it on.

"Sammy has this hat you'll like, though. A real Sherlock-Holmes-type hat, you know, checked and all. He wants a buck for it. I think he might give it to you for less. It's not worth a buck except to a guy who really likes hats."

"Cool," Charlie said. "That'd be cool. Some girl called you yesterday when you were at work."

Ack Ack opened his eyes. He took frequent cat naps throughout the day. It was the only thing that kept him going, he said. His teachers had warned him. Once more and out, they had said.

"A girl called up Ben?" he asked, incredulous. "What'd she want to sell him, life insurance or a magazine subscription?"

"Who was it?" Ben asked.

"She said it was Laurie."

"Laurie who?"

"How do I know? How many girls named Laurie do you know?" Charlie asked.

"Laurie is a very big name these days." Ben ticked off on his fingers. "There's Laurie Black, Laurie McIver and Laurie what's-her-name, the one who has her own Mustang. She has this fantastic red Mustang her father gave her for her birthday and she hardly knows how to drive. She sits behind the wheel and looks like she expects the thing to go up in smoke any minute. Can you imagine wasting a car like that on a stupe like her?"

"Her father must be loaded," Charlie said. "How come you don't ask her to the movies or something? That way, maybe she'd give you a shot at driving it."

"A similar thought had just occurred to me," Ack Ack said. "The price of two tickets to the movies is prohibitive, I agree, but with a shot at driving a Mustang as your reward, it might be worth it. I wouldn't even care what color it was," he added magnanimously.

"It's not worth it," Ben said. "She's a fool. She talks all the time and when she isn't talking, she's laughing. Ever since she had the braces taken off her teeth, she's always flapping those fangs in my face."

"That's all right," Ack Ack said. "Whenever the conversation slows down, you can always admire her orthodontia, ask how many thou it set her old man back, stuff like that."

"Ben! Charlie!"

"There's the old lady," Ben said, hunching his shoulders down into his jacket.

"I'm out of here," he said. "Tell Mom I had to go to the library to work on my term paper."

"Where are you really going?" Charlie asked.

"I probably will go to the library for a while. Then it's possible I might go to listen to a couple of albums at Ed Reilly's house."

"When your plans firm up, let me know," Ack Ack said. He looked as if he might drop off again at any minute.

"Listen, if I don't split now, my mother will have me painting the shutters and waxing the floors. Be a pal," Ben said to Charlie, "and divert Mom's attention while I make my getaway."

The telephone rang, and Charlie answered.

"Is Ben there?" a girl's voice said.

"It's for you," Charlie said.

"Yeah? Who's this? Oh, Laurie. Sure, hi." Ben looked at Charlie and Ack Ack through the buttonhole of his jacket. "I don't know. I think it's to read the first three chapters and make an outline of them. You'd better call someone else, though. I'm not absolutely sure that's right. O.K." He hung up.

"I'm out of here," he said again.

Ack Ack opened one eye. "I don't like to see you brushing off a chick who owns her own Mustang," he said. "That's pretty shortsighted of you."

"You want to get involved, you get involved," Ben said. "She's more your type anyway. Let's go."

Ack Ack got to his feet reluctantly. "I'm off to the madding crowd, kid," he said to Charlie. "Peace," and he shuffled after Ben.

bet you don't know how many feet you're supposed to park from a fire hydrant, Dad," Ben said. He had just got his driver's license. The sun had barely set on his sixteenth birthday last month before he had memorized the driver's manual and passed his driver's ed course.

"Listen, I've been driving for twenty-three years and I haven't had a ticket for parking too close to a fire hydrant yet," his father said.

"How many feet?" Ben pursued.

"It varies in different states," his father answered.

"I knew you didn't know," Ben said triumphantly. "Tell you what. I'm going to give you all a break. I'm going to take the whole family for a ride. Mom, Dad, Charlie, let the ace take over."

Charlie was in the car like a shot. He thought Ben was a cool driver. It took Mom and Dad a little longer.

Dad said he had some bills to pay; Mom said she was in the middle of a meat loaf; but eventually they were persuaded to hop aboard.

"Is there any kind of insurance for this kind of trip?" Dad muttered.

It was an unforgettable journey.

Ben and his father sat in front; Charlie and his mother in back, strapped in their seat belts as if they were going over Niagara Falls in a barrel. Before Ben turned the key in the ignition, his mother started putting on the brakes. She sat there in the back seat practically shoving her foot through the floor boards she was putting on the brakes so hard.

"Slower, slower," she yelled.

"I haven't even started," Ben said patiently. "Take it slow, Flo," he murmured under his breath. His mother's name was Beatrice.

"To the right, over to the right, you're driving too far over on the left," Dad shouted. Ben yanked the wheel over hard and almost ran into a parked car.

"Just go down to the light and take a right turn, then head for home," the old man said from between clenched teeth. "I don't think I'm up to this."

One thing about Ben, Charlie noticed, was that when he came to to a traffic light, he counted on its being green. If it wasn't, he put the car into first and drove about two miles an hour, hoping the light would change. It hurt his pride to bring the car to a full stop. It was against his principles.

15

As the happy family approached the red light, Ben shifted into second, then first. He inched his way down the street. Charlie's mother dug her fingers deep into his arm.

"For Pete's sake, Mom," Charlie hollered, "he's only doing five miles an hour. Cut it out! That hurts! Relax!"

The light remained red. Ben came to a grinding halt behind a car already stopped. Charlie tried to escape from his mother's clutching hands. She was faster than he. And stronger. She grabbed him and hung on. She was so busy putting her foot on the nonexistent brakes and moving her lips in prayer that she paid no attention to his cries.

"Benny boy, how's it going?" A creature in a giant crash helmet swooped around the corner, gunning the motor of his motorbike so he'd sound like a hotshot. It was Ack Ack.

"He looks like he's suited up for Sebring," Ben said admiringly.

Casually, no sweat, he took his hand off the wheel to salute his friend.

It was a fatal mistake. The engine coughed once, twice, and died. The light changed to green. The car behind Ben sounded its horn, then the one behind it did the same.

"Get a move on!" a voice shouted.

Ben had stalled. Beautifully, embarrassingly, he had stalled. He was holding up an entire line of cars. Before he could get the car going again, the light changed back to red. Cars pulled from behind him, forming a new line. Every driver gave him a dirty look. Ben, Charlie, the old folks all stared straight ahead.

A red Mustang with a girl driving pulled alongside Ben.

"Hey, Ben," she said, smiling, "you need some help?"

Charlie saw Ben's face flush. Even the tips of his ears were bright.

He waved his hand, shrugged his shoulders. "Just a little transmission trouble," he said. "I can handle it. Thanks anyway."

The Mustang pulled away. After an eternity, Ben got the car into gear. Unfortunately, he mistook third for first. The passengers rolled and tossed as if they were riding a ship during a storm in the North Atlantic. The two in the front seat almost went through the windshield. In the rear, Charlie felt a little seasick. He and his mother, safely encased in their seat belts, were bounced around like a couple of demented Yo-yos.

They rode the rest of the way in silence. Ben pulled up in front of the house. The parents debarked. They looked older than when they had started.

As they helped each other up the path and into the house, Ben said disgustedly, "My gosh, you'd never suspect Dad was a jet pilot in the war. What's he get so uptight about a little ride to the corner for? I wasn't going all that fast."

"Yeah," Charlie said, unfastening his seat belt. When he got out of the car, his legs felt a little rubbery. With

Ben at the wheel, everything seemed stepped up. There was something about the way he took a curve, something about the way he downshifted at every opportunity, about the way he approached a stop sign, the way he yielded when the sign said *Yield,* that made the whole business of driving with him a real adventure.

Muttering to himself, Ben went inside. Charlie sat down on the front steps to rest his legs and get his equilibrium back. To look busy and give himself a project, he went to work on the scab on his knee. Even it seemed a trifle pale after the ride with Ben. It really was a beauty, though. It was almost the exact shape of Texas. He planned to lift it off in one unbroken piece and present it, gift wrapped, to his friend Arthur, who hated scabs worse than anything. They made him sick to his stomach.

The last scab Charlie'd saved for Arthur had been shaped just like Florida. But at the crucial moment, when he was getting ready to lift off that one, Miami and Miami Beach had broken off. Somehow, it had never been the same after that.

As if he'd heard someone call his name, Arthur came around the corner of the house, legs churning, breathing hard.

"Made it in forty-two seconds this time," he panted, checking the second hand on his watch. Arthur lived three houses down from Charlie. He was always trying to better his time from portal to portal.

"What held you up?" Charlie asked, yawning. Charlie and Arthur had been best friends since they'd gone to the same nursery school and Charlie had been bounced because the lady who ran the school said he was a disruptive influence. That meant he was always picking a fight with Arthur or somebody. There was nothing Charlie liked better than a good squabble. The lady who ran the school was a personal friend of Arthur's mother so, naturally, Charlie had been kicked out. One of them had to go, the lady said.

Unfortunately, that same day their mother had had a call from Ben's teacher, saying he also was a disruptive influence and a nuisance and she couldn't cope with him. Was he a problem at home too?

Their mother had hung up the phone, put her head in her hands, and cried. She had failed, she said. Two sons and each of them a misfit in society. When their father heard that Charlie and not Arthur had been tossed out of nursery school, he called it favoritism, because Arthur's mother and the school head were friends. Then he settled down and gave Ben his special half-hour lecture on the values of education and toeing the line and facing up to Life and Responsibility. Ben knew large sections of the lecture by heart, he had heard it so often.

But now Ben was a junior in high school and a member of the Honor Society, and Charlie and Arthur were in the sixth grade at Broad River School. There was no Honor Society in the sixth grade, which was a break.

Arthur was much taller and weighed a lot more than Charlie but he didn't have as much muscle and he couldn't run anywhere near as fast. Charlie was small and considered himself wiry. He did twenty push-ups a night and was sure he detected a swelling in his biceps that had not been there before. He figured a small guy with muscles had more chance than a big flabby guy.

Arthur wrote poems which he read standing up in full view of Miss Peterson's English class. Charlie was so embarrassed on these occasions that he asked to be excused to go to the boy's room. But after the first few times, Miss Peterson caught on. She was much too smart for Charlie. She told him that in just those words.

"I'm much too smart for you," she said, smiling her cruel smile and clicking her teeth. Miss Peterson was engaged to be married, which was all right with Charlie. The sooner the better. Then maybe she'd have some kids of her own and she could smile her cruel smile at them and tell them how smart she was and not let them go to the boy's room either.

The last poem Arthur had written had been about spring and the daffodils coming up and the birds singing, and Charlie had been seized with a fit of coughing so violent that even Miss Peterson had said he could go to the fountain and get a drink. She probably thought he was going to choke to death and she didn't know how to explain it to the principal.

She stood at the door of the room and watched Charlie walk the entire length of the hall and watched while he bent over to get a drink. She stood there, tapping her foot, so he couldn't do anything but come straight back. He walked as slow as possible and finally she said, "Snap it up!" in a hissing voice like a snake.

Boy, do I feel sorry for the poor guy you're going to marry, Charlie said silently. He didn't want Miss Peterson to blow her stack the way she had the last time he'd said something she wasn't supposed to hear. His mother had had to come down to school and have a conference and everything.

Except for the fact that Arthur wrote poems and read them aloud to the class, he was a good kid. He laughed at Charlie's jokes about as hard as he laughed at his own, and there weren't too many kids who did that. They thought theirs were funnier. He also liked to eat a lot but his mother always had him on a diet so he gave Charlie a bunch of cupcakes and junk.

He usually had money too. His father gave him an allowance when he thought of it. When Charlie wanted to borrow, Arthur loaned him cash and didn't even charge interest, like some tightwad friends Charlie could mention, if he wanted.

"Artie, you are one in a million," Charlie said.

Arthur recognized the tone of voice. "I'm broke," he

said. "My mother's birthday was last week and the guy got a buck off me in church Sunday."

Charlie popped his eyeballs out so far they almost lay on his cheeks. He clutched his throat and rolled on the ground, making gagging noises.

"How come?" he asked when he could talk.

Arthur was pleased by the violence of the reaction. "I felt this thing in my pocket, all soft like an old sock," he said, "and I pulled it out and it was a dollar bill I didn't know I had and the guy passing the plate happened along just at the wrong moment, so what could I do?"

"You could've pretended you were having a fit or something," Charlie said. "I would've. Wow! Talk about lousy timing."

Both boys sat with their chins in their hands and thought about the fickle finger of fate.

Charlie picked at his scab, gently lifting first one corner, then the other corner. The skin underneath was pink. Things were coming along nicely.

"Cut that out," Arthur said, turning pale.

Charlie put his hands behind his head. He thought he'd take a tip from Ack Ack and catch a cat nap.

A quick trot around the yard made Arthur feel better. A poem began to form inside his head. It was extraordinary the way that happened, just when he least expected.

" 'Twas the first day of summer," Arthur recited aloud, "and birds were on the wing."

Blankness. Inspiration fled. Summer. Wing. What next?

He looked at Charlie. Asleep? At ten o'clock in the morning? "I am getting dumber, so I begin to sing."

He put his mouth next to Charlie's ear and sang a loud, clear, tuneless melody. Arthur was tone deaf.

Charlie barely stirred.

"The first day of summer," Arthur shouted, "you are getting dumber."

Charlie sat up. "You are a pain," he said crossly.

W ho's the chick?" Ben asked Ack Ack, who had stopped by to borrow some history notes.

"Thanks, old buddy," Ack Ack said, pocketing the notes. "You are a lifesaver. I don't know what I'd do without you. Our friendship knows no bounds. You are a prince of a fellow, Ben."

"Stop the rhetoric, pal," Ben said, "and tell me who the cool-looking chick is you've got sitting out there in your old man's car." Charlie looked out the window. Whoever it was, she looked like any other girl to him.

"That's no chick. That's only Penny. She gets a three-week spring vacation. How do you like that?"

Penny was Ack Ack's sister. She was a year younger than he and Ben. Last year Mr. Ackerman had sent her to a girl's boarding school. It cost a mint, her father said, but this outfit was not only devoted to things of the mind and of the spirit, but of the body as well.

Sports were a big part of the curriculum. They had everything covered.

"That's Penny?" Ben raised his eyebrows. "Not ole Penny the Pig?" Ben kept on peering from behind the curtains. "From what I can see she sure looks different."

Ack Ack scratched his head.

"She ain't," he said succinctly. "As bossy as ever. No sooner does she set foot inside the front door than she's telling me I better get a haircut. Get her. Only thing different about her is she must've lost about a hundred pounds. They really keep those dames hopping at that school. Field hockey, riding, tennis, you name it."

Penny had always been what Charlie's father called "a good substantial girl," which meant she was fat. Fat and bossy, that was some combination, Charlie figured. He remembered that Ben used to call her Captain Chubby.

"Maybe I better go and check her out," Ben said. "Say a fast welcome home or words to that effect."

"Make it snappy," Ack Ack said. "I've got to get to work."

Charlie went out to the car with Ben and Ack Ack.

"Hello, Ben," Penny said. She didn't say anything to Charlie, didn't even look at him. He felt invisible.

"How are you?" she said in that sugary phony tone Charlie had noticed girls used when they were talking to Ben and older kids. They never talked that way to him. He felt like popping a girl in the face who talked that way.

"Hey, Penny, how's the girl?" Ben leaned on the car. "I never would've known you. You've changed some."

Penny smiled. "I know," she said. She flipped her hair over her shoulders. Charlie figured she thought she was a Miss Teen Queen or one of those.

"How's school? You take over the joint yet? They elect you president of the student council or anything?" Ben asked.

Penny looked at herself in the rearview mirror. "I'm captain of the field hockey team," she said.

"Why not?" Charlie muttered. "With those legs."

"No kidding?" Ben laughed as if Penny had said something funny. "I hear you're going to be home for three weeks."

Penny smiled. "Why don't you drop by?" she said. "We can talk over old times."

"I might," Ben said. "I just might."

"Listen, I've got to split," Ack Ack said. "The old lady will put a wrist lock on me if I don't get the car back."

"Say," Ben said, rubbing his chin as they watched Ack Ack drive away, "she's pretty nice."

"She still looks like Captain Chubby to me," Charlie said sourly. "How come she talks in that disgusting voice?"

"She's some nice tomato," Ben said.

"Can we go to Sammy's tomorrow?" Charlie asked. "I want to see about that hat."

"I guess so," Ben said absent-mindedly.

Sammy, I brought my kid brother in for a look at your wares," Ben said. "Charlie, this is Sammy."

Ben had told Charlie that Sammy was pretty cross-eyed but he hadn't described how little tufts of hair grew out of his ears. They sort of made up for the fact that he had almost no hair on his head. Sammy was a very interesting-looking man.

"Pleased to meet you, Charlie. You look like about a size twelve, fourteen, somewheres around there." Sammy backed off and sized Charlie up. "A rangy kid, you got a lot of growing in you yet, it's plain to see. An athletic type, like your brother here."

Sammy raised a finger. "Wait," he said. "One minute. I have something special, a real number for your inspection, Ben." He raced into the back where he kept his choicest items, not for sale to the average customer, only for favorites such as Ben.

"What do you think?" Sammy asked, coming back with something black over his arm.

"What is it?" Charlie asked.

"It's a tail coat," Sammy said. "Probably a custom-made job. The man who sold it to me, he was a waiter or a magician, something along those lines. A very expensive item. I can let you have it for a fraction of its original cost."

"Neat," said Ben, "but where would I wear it?"

"Where would you wear it? Where would you wear it?" Sammy threw his hands in the air. "What kind of a question is that? You'd wear it to a formal occasion, maybe to church or to a fancy-dress ball. All kinds of places."

Sammy stroked the black material lovingly. "I always wanted one of these when I was your age. You got one of these items, you can go anywhere."

Ben put the tail coat on and stood in front of the full-length mirror Sammy kept in the store for just such events. He looked a little lost. The coat had been made for a much bigger man.

"It just so happens I got this to go along with it and I am not averse to throwing it in for gratis," and Sammy placed a top hat, slightly the worse for wear but still a top hat, on Ben's head.

"That's one hundred per cent silk," he said softly.

Charlie breathed heavily.

"Boss," he said, "really boss."

"I don't know," Ben said. "It feels sort of funny."

"Listen, a top hat's not something you just put on and feel right in. Believe me"—and Sammy's eyes seemed to collide over the bridge of his nose—"believe me, when you own one of them, you are a man of the world. A *bon vivant*, an entrepreneur, even a tycoon. But it comes gradual. You got to take it easy. You got to adjust to it slow."

The sun shone through the dirty windows of the shop. A train went by, rattling the cast-off golf clubs and wooden skis that someone had unloaded on Sammy. An old tiger cat looked sullenly from behind a chair.

"And I believe I might, just might, don't count on it, have something to go with your outfit. Stay here. Don't move," and Sammy sped away again into the back.

"He's a character," Charlie said.

"One of nature's noblemen," Ben agreed. Sammy came back carrying a package wrapped in tissue paper.

"What is it?" Charlie asked again.

"It's spats, clod," Ben said when Sammy had taken the paper off. "Don't you know spats when you see 'em?"

"I never saw a pair before," Charlie said.

Ben slipped the gray felt harnesses over his desert boots. The effect was astonishing.

"Do they add the final touch or do they add the final touch?" Sammy wanted to know. "With them gaiters on you could go to Buckingham Palace even."

"Who needs Buckingham Palace?" Ben did a little dance. The spats did indeed look fine. "I might just wear them to the movies. I might even sport the whole schmeer."

"How are you going to get out of the house without Mom's seeing you?" Charlie asked. "You know what she'd say."

"I'll take care of the old lady," Ben said masterfully. "I can handle her."

"Oh yeah?" Charlie nudged Ben. "How about the hat? Ask about the hat."

"Right. Sammy, Charlie here is interested in purchasing a Sherlock-Holmes-type hat. I told him you had one you might consider an offer on."

Sammy laid a finger alongside his nose. His left eye seemed to be keeping track of it.

"The checked one," he said. "A good buy at a buck. Not a hole in it, not a mark on it. I don't think I can let it go for less than a buck."

Charlie said, "I don't have a buck."

"How much you got?"

"I have twenty-seven cents," Charlie said. "I could let you have that as a down payment. I could pay you a little each week."

"If I let you have it for fifty cents, that makes it too easy," Sammy thought aloud. "Suppose we shake on seventy-five. For seventy-five you got yourself a buy. A beautiful buy. I, Sammy, do not lie."

Charlie and Sammy shook on it.

"It's a deal," Charlie said. "Can I wear it now?"

"Ordinarily, I do not allow a customer to wear the merchandise until it is fully paid for," Sammy said. "In this case, I will make an exception. You are a relative of Ben here and I know you are as good as your word. You may wear it out of my store after I receive my deposit of twenty-seven cents."

Charlie thrashed through his pockets and came up with a quarter and a penny.

"I thought I had twenty-seven," he said, turning both pockets inside out.

Sammy raised his hand. "Never mind," he said. "Sammy does not go back on his word. I am an honest man. For a twenty-six-cent deposit you may wear your purchase out of my store. Good will is everything. I been creating good will among my customers for more years than I like to think about."

Sammy and Charlie shook hands again.

"Done and done," Sammy said.

"What's 'done and done' mean?" Charlie asked when he and Ben were on their way home.

"He got it out of the movies. He told me all the guys in the movies he saw when he was a kid were always saying it when they were going to fight a duel or something."

"But what's it mean?"

"I don't know." Ben shrugged. "What difference does it make? It sounds good. Some things you don't want to investigate too thoroughly, kid. Some things you just accept."

"Done and done," said Charlie. His new hat gave him a feeling of power that was very pleasant, very pleasant indeed.

"I need a pipe to go with this," he told Ben. "Sherlock Holmes always smoked a pipe."

"Yeah, well, that comes later. Try the old lady and the old man with the hat first."

"What about the tail coat and the top hat and the spats?" Charlie asked. "That'll really have them flipping."

"Sammy's going to hold them for me. For six bucks. I plan to bring them home separately. That way they won't get hit with the works all at once."

"Good idea," Charlie said. "Done and done."

L et's hitch a ride home," Charlie suggested.

"Naw," Arthur said. "It's against the law."

A long shiny car pulled up to the curb. "Hey, you kids, no loitering now." The deep voice sounded right in Charlie's ear. Arthur turned pale.

"All's we were doing is standing on the corner," Arthur said.

It was Ack Ack, laughing up a storm. He looked over his left shoulder, then over his right. No one was following him. Good.

"I really had you going, didn't I? Thought I was the fuzz, didn't you? Oh, yeah. Hop in, comrades, and I'll give you a lift."

Charlie and Arthur hopped in.

"How come you get to drive your father's car?" Charlie asked. Ack Ack was usually on his motorbike. His father had this shiny car and he treated it like it was Apollo 15 or something. He was prouder of that car than anything. He washed and waxed it so much that when the sun hit it, the reflection was blinding.

"My old man's away on a business trip," Ack Ack said, "and you know my mother. She's very permissive. She said I could drive it today if I picked up Penny when I got out of school and saved her a trip. O.K. with you guys if I make a brief *sortie* into the fleshpots?"

"Sure," Charlie said. He'd never been to the fleshpots, whatever they were, but they sounded worth seeing.

The fleshpots turned out to be Murray's, the local department store. Penny was standing in front, frowning.

"Where have you been?" she asked Ack Ack crossly. "I've been waiting for hours."

"The fresh air's good for you," Ack Ack said.

"A gentleman would open the door for me," Penny said, opening her own door.

"One thing I have never claimed to be," Ack Ack said proudly, "and that's a gentleman."

Penny turned and surveyed Charlie and Arthur.

"You kids look like something the cat dragged in," she said without preamble. "When was the last time you took a bath?"

"A week ago Saturday," Charlie said. "My mother's very strict. She makes me take a bath every other week."

Penny directed a stare of considerable malevolence at him. "You always were a smart aleck," she said.

Arthur tittered and poked Charlie in the ribs.

"Turn left at Oak Street," Penny said. "I want to see if the Thompsons still live there."

"Say 'please,'" Ack Ack said.

"Where's Ben?" she asked Charlie. She didn't say "please," he noticed.

"He works at the B and T after school."

"What does he do there?" she asked.

"Oh, lots of things. Pumps gas, does repairs. He can do practically anything. The guy says Ben's the best worker he's ever had."

"I thought he had a job at the ice-cream place," Arthur said.

"He did but he got fired. He was overloading the cones and the profits were 'way down."

"Drive over to the B and T and let's get the tank filled," Penny said. "We can charge it to Dad."

"Are you kidding me?" Ack Ack whispered in a loud voice. "I value my life too much for that, sister. Anyway, I have to get home and take my bike to the shop. It's making funny noises."

"So what else is new?" Penny said, combing her hair.

"Why don't you get off my back?" Ack Ack said.

They pulled up into the Ackerman's driveway.

"We'll walk from here," Charlie said. "Thanks for the lift."

Ack Ack got out of the car and went into the house. Penny slid over to the driver's seat. She turned the key in the ignition. The engine purred. She checked herself in the mirror.

"You can't drive," Charlie said from the back seat. "You're too young."

"That's all you know." Penny smiled at herself. "I've been driving for ages. Not on the road, just in the driveway, for practice. It's a cinch. See?"

Mesmerized, Charlie and Arthur stayed in the back seat. Penny put the car in reverse. She backed up. A loud screech of brakes sounded and a man shouted, shook his fist, and zigzagged just enough to miss hitting the car.

"You pulled out too far," Arthur said weakly. "You're in the road."

"You didn't look," Charlie said. "Wow! That was close."

"I think maybe you'd better put the car in the garage," Arthur suggested.

Penny ran the comb through her hair. "Right," she said.

She put the car into drive. It glided smoothly up the driveway into the garage and kept on going.

"Put the brakes on, you dim-wit!" Charlie yelled. Arthur covered his head with his arms and said nothing.

At the last minute, just before the car went out the other end, Penny put on the brakes. Rakes, ladders and stacked firewood bruised the shiny surface, and all was still.

Penny wet her lips and looked in the mirror. Arthur sat with his hands over his eyes. Charlie said, "Let me out of here while I can still walk."

They inspected the damage. Not too bad. A few nicks and scrapes that could be touched up.

"You were lucky," Charlie said. "You might've gone right out the other end."

Ack Ack stood there, wringing his hands. "She did it, not me," he said over and over. "What'll Dad say? He'll think it was me. I better run away from home. Tell Mom to forward my mail."

"Ben can fix it," Charlie said. "He can fix just about anything."

For the first time, Penny looked at Charlie and smiled. "Good idea," she said. "Let's call him up."

A car that sounded as if it had no muffler stopped at the curb. Looking very sharp in his red vest, black shirt, and striped pants, Ben got out. "Thanks," he said to the driver. The car sped away.

"You got here just in time, Benny boy. A most fortuitous moment for your arrival," Ack Ack said. "We have a problem."

"She almost killed us," Charlie said. "She almost ran her father's car through the wrong end of the garage."

Ben laughed. "Just like a dame," he said. Penny smiled at him.

"Come on in and have a Coke," she said. Always ready for refreshment, Charlie and Arthur went along.

"I didn't mean you two," she said when she discovered they had followed her into the kitchen.

"Hey, she's not as fat as she used to be but she's just as bossy," Charlie whispered in a loud tone.

38

Penny got three Cokes out of the refrigerator. "You kids will have to split one," she said, flipping her hair over her shoulders. "Let's go into the den where we can talk in private," she said to Ben.

"Hey," Charlie said, "I didn't know you had a den. I thought only bears and lions and like that had dens."

"That brother of yours is a laugh a minute," Penny said.

"Yeah," Ben agreed. "Listen, tell me about your school. You must get awful bored, surrounded by nothing but girls all day long, no dates or anything like that."

"Oh," Penny said, "we have lots of boys' schools near us. We have dances and things with them. Actually the social life is a heck of a lot more active than it is around here."

Sometimes it didn't pay to eavesdrop. Charlie made throwing-up noises, flexed his muscles, and punched Arthur a couple of times. Not hard.

"Cut it out," Arthur said crossly. "You and your muscles."

"Let's go in the den and chew the fat, Artie," Charlie cooed.

The door to the den slammed loudly.

"I've got a whole bunch of things I want to tell you," Charlie said in falsetto. "But first let me borrow your comb. My hair's a mess."

"It doesn't look any worse than usual," Arthur said.

On Saturday, Charlie leaped out of bed and did twice the number of push-ups he did on weekdays. Then he stood in front of the mirror and forced the blood into his veins by holding his breath and sticking his neck out as far as it would go. This produced a set of the most impressive veins Charlie had ever seen. Fat and thick and blue, they looked like the Amazon on a map. They were some powerful veins, all right. It was too bad there was no one else to admire them. It wasn't every guy in the sixth grade with a set of veins like those.

Charlie did some deep knee bends and ran in place for a few minutes, making guttural noises and shouting unintelligible words like the pro-football players do on TV.

"Hey, cut the racket!" Ben shouted from his room. "Let a guy sleep, will ya?"

Charlie looked at the clock. It was already twenty past six. What the heck was the matter with Ben anyway? Charlie could remember not so long ago when Ben was always first out of bed. Now he slept half the day away. He must be getting soft in his old age. One thing was certain: Charlie wasn't going to let himself get old and soft.

His physical-fitness program over, Charlie sat down and wrote a letter to Camp Pilot asking them to please send him the informative brochure they had advertised in last Sunday's paper. This camp not only offered a program of professional flight instruction plus ground school which would qualify him for a private pilot's license, it also offered hiking, mountain climbing, and water sports. That was a lot of camp for the money, although there was no mention in the ad of how much anything cost.

As a postscript, Charlie said "Please send me a complete price list." The first thing his father would say when Charlie brought up the subject of Camp Pilot would be, "How much?" It had been Charlie's experience that when price was not mentioned in print, it meant "Watch out."

Charlie closed his eyes and imagined himself on his first solo flight. A smile played across his face as he felt the engine responding to his touch. He was halfway across the Atlantic when he had to turn back for fuel. Somebody had goofed. Heads would roll.

Excitement always made Charlie hungry. He tiptoed

downstairs, eased the refrigerator door open, and leaned into the crisp and frigid air. If his mother wasn't asleep, she would yell, "Shut that refrigerator!" She could hear the door opening even if she was running the vacuum cleaner.

Not much there. A roast for tomorrow, some eggs, a couple of covered dishes that probably had green fuzz covering whatever lay underneath. His mother was an expert on growing fuzz on things. His father called it her green thumb.

Arthur's face pressed against the back door, his breath fogging the glass. He looked sleepy but he could hear that refrigerator door opening as clearly as Charlie's mother.

"Get lost," Charlie directed.

Arthur took this to be an invitation and came in. He leaned over Charlie's shoulder.

"Is that chocolate pudding?" he asked. "And a jar of herring?" He smelled of peanut butter.

"No, it's spinach," Charlie said. Arthur liked to ask questions he already knew the answers to.

The dish of pudding had been around for a while. It had started to shrink away from the sides of the bowl. That was how you could tell.

"Do you think your mother'd mind if I polished off the pudding and the herring?" Arthur asked. He had very good manners. He never ate anything without asking permission.

Charlie threw his shoulders back and tucked his fists in, the way guys did in muscle-building ads.

42

"Naw, she won't mind," Charlie said. She probably wouldn't. She didn't believe in throwing away what she called "perfectly good food," even if the food was starting to shrink. Arthur was very useful when it came to cleaning out the refrigerator. About the only thing he wouldn't eat was the green fuzz.

"My muscles are getting so big I might get stuck going through our front door," Charlie confided. "You know why they stick out so far? Push-ups, that's why. You ought to try 'em." He was always trying to get Arthur to build up his body. "You're not in very good shape," he said.

"Fat runs in my family," Arthur said proudly, the way other kids might say "Brains run in my family" or "blue eyes" or "big noses." Arthur was proud of the fat that ran in his family.

"You drag too much weight around, you'll have a heart attack," Charlie warned.

"No kidding?" Arthur unwrapped a Hershey Bar.

"You ever see veins like that?" Charlie thrust his neck and wrists toward Arthur. "Look at those if you want to see some veins."

Arthur looked away. He didn't particularly like things like veins and arteries and stuff like that. He knew they were necessary, but that didn't mean he had to like looking at them.

"You ought to see Ben lift his bar bells," Charlie said. "He just picks 'em up like they were a bag of feathers. He is some powerful guy."

"He doesn't look so powerful to me," Arthur said.

Sometimes he got tired of hearing how great Ben was. To hear Charlie tell it, Ben was the smartest, strongest, funniest guy in the world. Arthur did not have a brother to brag about. He wished he had.

"For his size, he is extremely powerful," Charlie said firmly. "You should see his muscles. They're terrific. And you ought to see him work out on the parallel bars. Wow!" Charlie rolled his eyes back in his head. "I only hope I'm as strong as he is when I get to be his age. Not to mention as smart, in the Honor Society and all."

"If he's so smart," Arthur said, "how come he's going out with ole Penny the Pig? My mother said she saw them at the movies last night. Tell me that. Just tell me that."

He had him there. From the expression on Charlie's face, Arthur knew he had him there.

"If he's so smart," Arthur pursued, crowing, "how come he takes out that dope, huh?"

"She's pretty good-looking, now that she got skinny," Charlie said. How did he get pushed into defending somebody he hated the way he hated Penny? That made him mad.

"Would you take a girl like her out?" Arthur asked.

"Me? I wouldn't take any girl out. I'm the wrong guy to ask. That is the dumbest thing I ever heard of," Charlie said disgustedly. "You have just hit rock bottom, plain old rock bottom when you say things like that."

"O.K., O.K.," Arthur said hastily. He didn't want

Charlie to blow a gasket. "Listen, I made up a new poem. See what you think." He stood up and closed his eyes. He could only recite standing up with his eyes closed.

"Chris Columbus said the world was round, with good ideas he did abound."

He stopped.

"Yeah," Charlie said. "Go on." He secretly liked it when Arthur asked his opinion on poetry.

"That's all. I couldn't think of any more words to rhyme."

Charlie found a bag of potato chips in the cupboard. He gave Arthur a handful. "I don't call that a poem," he said, spraying crumbs. "I can do as good as that."

He thought a minute.

"Chris Columbus sailed the seven seas, looking for a bag of fleas."

"Hey neat," Arthur said.

Charlie smiled, lay down on the kitchen floor, and did ten more push-ups without even breathing hard.

Arthur looked at his watch. "I've got to go," he said. "It's time for breakfast."

"You can eat here if you want. Nobody's up but me."

"What's for chow?"

"I could make some pancakes," Charlie said. The last time Arthur had stayed for breakfast, Charlie made pancakes and each one had lain like a lead bullet at the bottom of Arthur's stomach all day long.

"I don't know," he said slowly.

"How about a jelly sandwich?" Charlie asked.

Arthur made a face. He wasn't all that hot on jelly sandwiches.

"What kind of jelly?" he asked.

Charlie got the jar down from the shelf.

"Currant," he said.

Arthur looked relieved.

"O.K.," he conceded, "just so long as it isn't grape."

How about meeting me after school today and going down to Sammy's for a fast check to see what he has?" Charlie asked. He was sitting on the edge of the bathtub watching Ben decide whether he needed a shave or not. He had shaved last week. Maybe it was time for another scrape job.

"I can't," Ben said, inspecting his upper lip.

"Why not?"

"I told Penny I'd go to her house and take a look at her father's car to see if I can patch it up before he gets home. The guys at B and T said they'd give me the putty and the paint. I helped them paint a car last week and it's not hard."

"How much you going to charge her?"

"Don't be a boob. I'm not going to charge her anything," Ben said.

"You got to be kidding me," Charlie said, twisting the

brim of his Sherlock Holmes hat to the left. "Since when are you doing jobs like that for nothing? Since when, is what I want to know. Boy, times sure have changed around here."

Charlie yawned elaborately and tightened the green-and-orange muffler around his neck. Sammy had given him the muffler gratis and it was a beauty. It was so long Charlie had to wrap it around his neck quite a few times so it wouldn't drag on the floor. There weren't too many mufflers around as cool as this one.

"You won't see yourself coming and going in that, I can tell you," Charlie's mother had said when he showed it to her.

"You know it, Mom," he had agreed.

"You were over at Penny's house last night too, and Mom nearly blew a fuse. She thought you were doing your homework and when she went into your room and found you had skinned out, she was burned up," Charlie said.

"You told her, I suppose? You're getting to be a regular little brown noser, aren't you?" Ben asked scornfully.

"I did not tell," Charlie said indignantly. "She came up to put some sheets away or something. What do you think I am, some kind of a stool pigeon?"

"I just went over for a couple of seconds to hear some of her records. She has a very interesting collection of records. Where's that shirt Grandma gave me for Christmas?" and Ben started to burrow through his drawers.

48

"What shirt? How do I know? You mean that white shirt? The one you said you wouldn't wear on a bet?"

Ben ignored him. "I know it's here somewhere," he said.

"How come ole Penny the Pig is so fascinating all of a sudden? Outside of the fact that she's skinny instead of fat, she looks the same to me. And her personality sure is the same. I don't get it. The Pig is a big deal all of a sudden. . . ."

"Watch your mouth, kid," Ben said softly. He put an armlock on Charlie. It didn't really hurt but a little pressure would make all the difference. "Just watch what you say." Ben's voice was angry and his eyes were not smiling the way they usually were.

Charlie broke away.

"You don't have to start throwing your muscles around, either," he said. "You think you're some kind of a strong-arm guy, like in the Mafia."

"She's changed," Ben said. "She's really nice. She's grown up a lot."

"You used to think she was a fink. I remember you said she was one. And when she asked you to her party you made up a big lie about how you had a toothache and had to go to the dentist. That was only last year. And how about calling her Captain Chubby?"

"That wasn't last year," Ben said. "It was about a year and a half ago."

"O.K., so it was a year and a half. She's a bigger boss than ever. You should have heard her giving Ack Ack orders in the car the other day. She sounded like a drill sergeant," Charlie said.

Ben started to whistle under his breath. He had found the white shirt and now he tucked it into his gray flannel slacks, which had been bought before he had started to really grow and were too short now.

"You look like you're going to a funeral dressed like that," Charlie said. "You look like a square."

Ben put on a pair of brown loafers.

Charlie let his arms hang down until the blood swelled his veins.

"You're going out of the house in those?" he asked. "I thought you said only straight arrows wore loafers. Where'd you get them?"

"I borrowed them from Ed Reilly," Ben said.

"Boy, if only Sammy could see you now. He'd think you were some kind of a traitor, I bet."

"What if he did? I'm tired of looking like a bum. If a guy feels like looking decent, he ought to be allowed to without some people making a Federal case out of it," Ben said angrily.

"I can hear Sammy laughing from here," Charlie said. "Are you going there any more at all? How about that coat he's holding for you? Don't think plenty of other guys wouldn't like to get their mitts on that tail coat. Don't think that. You're some pal. He could've got a lot more dough for it too. He gave you a bargain. He must've had about a thousand people in there trying to get it off him and he told them No, he was saving

50

it for a special customer." Charlie ran out of breath. "You make me sick," he said finally.

Ben looked at him coldly. "Don't blow your mind on my account," he said.

"Maybe Mom would let you have some of her perfume to put behind your ears," Charlie said.

"Give me a break." Ben started to put on his black fedora, then hung it back on the bedpost. "Just give me a break."

Charlie turned his hat around and tightened the muffler. The Boston Strangler had finally caught up with him. When his head started to pound and the spots in front of his eyes got so numerous he lost count, he loosened his bonds. "You're going to need one," he said when he could talk.

"What?"

"A break, that's what."

Charlie looked at himself in the mirror. A pipe would be perfect, he thought. A pipe would really add the finishing touch. What was the use of having a hat like this without a pipe too?

Where's the big brother?" Sammy asked. "I haven't seen Ben for a month of Sundays. I hope his health is all right."

"He's O.K.," Charlie said. "It's just that he's tied up with this girl and she doesn't like him to dress like a bum. She wants him to look like a dude or something with a white shirt and all."

"I might have known," Sammy said sadly. "At his age, this is not uncommon. You got a girl friend, she doesn't like you to wear orange pants, you don't wear 'em. She doesn't want you to play poker, you don't play. She doesn't like you to have a night out with the boys, drink a few beers, have a few laughs, you stay home. I seen it happen ten, twenty, a thousand times."

He went into the back room and took the tail coat off a rack. "I guess I should offer this for sale. Ben will not be wanting it now. Too bad. It is such a beautiful garment." He patted it lovingly.

"Why don't you keep it yourself?" Charlie asked. "If you always wanted a tail coat, why not this one?"

Sammy stood still. He thought a minute.

"If I started buying my own merchandise, I would be out of business in no time at all. Just the other day I came across a lovely sweater, one hundred per cent pure cashmere. Soft! I got two dollars for it.

"How about a cup of tea?" Sammy asked suddenly. "It is just about that time in the afternoon. Would you care to join me?"

Charlie said, "Sure." Ordinarily, he wouldn't be caught dead drinking a cup of tea but here, with Sammy, everything was different.

Sammy put the Back in Ten Minutes sign on his door and turned the key in the lock.

"Just settle yourself down," he said to Charlie, nodding at a big old broken-down armchair, "and I'll have it going pronto." He had a little burner, a kettle, and a teapot in the back room. He even had a tiny refrigerator that he kept milk and butter and a couple of cigars in.

"Keeps them from going stale," he explained. "I like a good cigar."

The water started to boil. "Would you like a saltine or a graham cracker?" he asked. "I got cream cheese to go with it."

The old tomcat crawled out of a box of rags and rubbed against Sammy's legs. "He knows when it's time to put the feed bag on," Sammy said. "He is a very smart cat."

He put a saucer of milk down on the floor. "A pause

in the day's occupations," Sammy said. "You know that poem?"

"No," said Charlie. "But I have a friend, his name is Arthur. He probably knows it. He makes up poems himself, right out of his head. He says he doesn't know where they come from, they just pop in."

"I would like to meet your friend Arthur. Bring him down," Sammy said. "You know the one about young Lochinvar or 'Paul Revere's Ride,' to name a couple of my favorites? I am a lover of poetry."

Charlie shook his head.

"No!" Sammy looked shocked. "You are missing a treat," he said. Putting his hand inside his vest, he recited:

> *"Oh, young Lochinvar is come out of the west,*
> *Through all the wide border his steed was the*
> *   best;*
> *And, save his good broadsword, he weapon had*
> *   none,*
> *He rode all unarmed, and he rode all alone."*

He paused for breath. "From *Marmion* by Sir Walter Scott. These are great stories about great men. So they rhyme, that put a lot of people off. Take my advice. Read poetry. Lemon or cream?"

"Both," Charlie said to be polite.

"I do not think you would like both together. Try a little lemon on your first go round and then you can have cream in your second cup."

Charlie helped himself to sugar in liberal quantities and sat back with a graham cracker.

"It is too bad," Sammy said, drinking his tea, "that Ben has not found himself a girl friend who takes him as he is. It is also too bad that we will no longer be friends. I am sorry about that." His eyes looked very sad.

"Ben's not friends with anybody any more," Charlie said. "My mother says he is bewitched. She says at this rate he will get bounced out of the Honor Society."

"Oh, oh," Sammy said. "That is more bad news. Try another cup, with cream this time."

Charlie had two more cups of tea and a batch of saltines with cream cheese. That was a pretty good combination.

Someone knocked on Sammy's door.

"Ignore," he said. "They want to get in bad enough, they'll come back."

"It's been more than ten minutes since you put that sign up," Charlie ventured.

"I am my own boss," Sammy said. It was funny but after a while you got so used to Sammy's crossed eyes, you didn't even think about them any more.

"I am my own boss, and that is a very nice thing to be," he said. "I will never be a Mr. Vanderfeller but I open when I want, I close likewise. Besides, my customers are not run-of-the-mill people. They come in here, they know I am fair. I build up good will. Let's face it, they don't like me for my good looks."

"It's nice here," Charlie said after a silence, "but I guess I better get home. My mother told me to come home right after school. She worries when I'm not on time."

Sammy nodded. "Mine was the same," he said. "Still, at my age, she wants to know did I take my vitamin pills, how is the condition of my chest. It is true of mothers that they worry a lot. There is not too much you can do about it."

"Thanks for the tea," Charlie said, shaking hands.

"Don't mention it," Sammy said. "Tell Ben I will reimburse his down payment. Tell him I got two, three customers, they're dying to get their hands on a silk hat, never mind a tail coat in reasonably good condition. These items are in short supply at the moment. They bring good money."

"Done and done," Charlie said.

"And bring your friend the poet. I got a couple volumes of poetry he might like to peruse. Tell him if he would like to exchange a few thoughts, I am willing and able."

Sammy's eyes bounced together, then separated. "I always welcome company," he said.

"Right." Charley saw by the clock on the church tower that it was later than he thought. He hotfooted it for home.

Halfway down the street he turned around. Sammy was standing in front of his store, shading his eyes against the sun. He lifted his hand in salute. Charlie waved back. Then Sammy took the Back in Ten Minutes sign off his door and went inside.

went to see Sammy yesterday," Charlie said. Ben didn't answer. He was concentrating on rolling a cigarette. It wasn't easy but perseverance and practice were paying off. He was getting better. The cigarettes he rolled tasted terrible—Charlie knew from trying one puff—but they were a lot cheaper than buying a pack and then too, he got a sense of accomplishment from doing it. When Ben lit up a hand-rolled job and flicked ashes into the dirty glass that served as an ash tray, he got a feeling of well-being.

"Yeah?" he finally said. "How is he?"

"He's fine. He said to tell you you can have your deposit back any time. He said a lot of guys want to buy the tail coat."

"I wasn't worried about the dough. I know Sammy's a good guy. You never have to worry about Sammy."

Ben got off his bed and stood in front of the mirror, cigarette drooping from one corner of his mouth. He had on the bottoms to a pair of black-satin pajamas his grandmother had given his father for Christmas.

"Too rich for my blood," his father had said when he opened them.

"Then how about giving them to me?" Ben had asked. "They're not too rich for mine. Do you realize I don't own a pair of pajamas? Suppose I was in an accident and the hospital called up and said, 'Bring down Ben's toothbrush and pajamas.' Just suppose. It would be very embarrassing to say, 'He doesn't have any pajamas.' It would be very embarrassing for you."

His father had handed over the black-satin pajamas. "You're right," he said. "I don't think I could face it. And I know your mother couldn't. Save these for that unexpected trip to the hospital."

"There's only one thing the matter with them," Ben said after the first wearing, "and it's that they're so slippery I fall out of bed when I've got them on. I must've fallen out about five times last night."

Today he wore his red vest with no shirt underneath. He was working out with his bar bells. Panting and out of breath, he finally put them down.

"Wrap these around the old biceps, kid," he said, handing a tape measure to Charlie, "and let's see how I'm coming along."

"Exactly eleven and three-quarters inches," Charlie said, measuring.

Ben's face fell.

"That's what it was last week. And the week before. I have hit an impasse. I am doomed to be an undernourished weakling. On the other hand," Ben said, "brawn isn't everything."

"Right," said Charlie, "but it sure helps."

Ben took his vest off and put on his white shirt.

"That shirt doesn't have time to cool off, you wear it so much," Charlie said.

"You heard Mom say that," Ben said. "She thinks just because I wear a shirt one day it's dirty. I can get two, three days out of it."

He put his gray flannels over the black-satin pajama bottoms which hung only a little below the flannels. It made a sort of interesting effect, Charlie thought.

"You look like some kind of a nut," Charlie said. "You look like you are about forty years old or something, like a businessman."

Ben slipped his bare feet into Ed Reilly's loafers. "I'm out of here," he said.

"Where you going?"

"To the store for the old lady."

"In those clothes I thought you had a date with Penny the P—with Penny. I'm coming too."

"No you're not."

"Who's going to stop me? It's not your car."

"You know it. I wouldn't drive a lousy little-old-lady-type car like that. When I get a car, it's going to be a Porsche, a car that can do about a hundred and twenty miles per with no sweat." Ben kicked the drawer of his bureau closed.

"Come on if you want but it's going to be boring. I'm just going to the A & P."

He put his Bogie hat on. "Let's cut out before Mom gives us a bon voyage party," he said. He tilted the hat over one eye.

They tiptoed through the kitchen and ran into the garage and almost had it made. Then their mother popped out the back door.

"Boys," she yelled so that the whole neighborhood could hear, "don't forget those seat belts."

"Don't worry, Mom, we're all set," Ben said, backing out the drive.

She didn't trust them. She had to come over to the car, peer in, and test the belts to make sure they were fastened properly. Then came the worst part. They hoped nobody was watching. She stood wringing her hands and shouting instructions as they pulled out of the driveway and into the wasteland of Huckleberry Drive, which was where they lived.

Cupping her hands around her mouth, she hollered, "His life is in your hands," and "Don't forget, you are carrying precious cargo" and other equally embarrassing things.

"I get the impression that if it was just me, I could drive over a cliff and she wouldn't care," Ben said. "It's you she worries about."

Charlie waved and they eluded her and were off, the wind whistling through their hair. They were free.

Looking neither to the right or to the left, Ben kept his hands on the wheel in a racing driver's position—as if they were the hands of a clock reading ten minutes to two. This gave the driver the maximum control over the car, Ben had read somewhere, and it had made an indelible impression.

Ben was careful to observe the speed limit according to road conditions. He said, "Notice the old speedometer registers right on the button. Notice also my control over this 'bile."

"I wish I had a hat like that. It is cool," Charlie said.

"I know," Ben answered. "It is a Bogie hat. A good-luck hat. I can do anything I want, be anybody I want, when I have it on."

He circled the block and drove slowly down the street.

"Where are you going? I thought you said you were going to the store."

"I am. I just thought maybe Penny would like to go for a spin. I just thought I'd check and see if she was around."

"You should've told me," Charlie said. "If I'd known she was coming, I would've stayed home. Forget it. She is such a gross-out I . . ."

Ben slammed on the brakes.

"Cool it," he said. "You don't like who I give rides to, butt out, kid."

"Hi," Penny said. She just happened to be coming down her front path.

She leaned on the car window. She had on long

earrings that swung against her cheeks. "Where'd you get the hat?" she asked, wrinkling her nose.

"You like it? It's a Bogie hat, a good-luck charm."

She laughed and Charlie wanted to punch her in the nose more than he had ever wanted to do anything.

"It's too much," she said. "Absolutely too much."

"How come you're wearing those?" Charlie pointed to the earrings. "They're too fancy for the daytime. And how come you've got that stuff on your eyes?"

"Where are you going?" she asked Ben, ignoring Charlie's questions. She stared at his ears. He figured she was checking to see if they were dirty.

"Just to the store. Hop in." Ben leaned over and opened the door on Charlie's side.

"I don't think there's room for three of us," Penny said sweetly. "I'll sit in back."

She stood there looking at the ends of her long hair, smiling, smiling.

"O.K., so get in back," Charlie said.

"Out," Ben jerked his thumb at Charlie. "He's young," he said to Penny. "He'll learn. Get in back," he directed Charlie.

Charlie got out of the car and slammed the door. "I just remembered I have something to do," he said.

"Open the door for her," Ben said, his face red, his smile growing stiff on his face.

Penny flicked her hair over her shoulders.

"Let her open it herself. She's a big strong girl," Charlie said, stalking off.

He heard the car pull away, tires squealing, but he didn't turn around. The taste of the last word was not nearly as sweet as it was cracked up to be.

Ack Ack stopped by the next day to see if Ben had finished work.

"No, he's not here," Charlie said, "but come on in. I've got a couple of things I want to ask you."

"Ask away," Ack Ack said, draping himself around the stove.

"What happens if Ben and Penny decide to get married or something?" Charlie blurted out.

Ack Ack looked even more mournful than usual.

"The way I figure it, that might ruin a beautiful friendship," he said after some thought. "She's my sister, right? I know her bloodlines are of the finest, right? She has a dowry of a hundred clams my grandmother left her and a couple of crummy tablecloths in an old hope chest. She's also got a lousy disposition, but she's not too bad-looking now that she shed all that flesh. She says she's going to be a zoologist and I understand zoologists make good money."

"What's a zoologist?" Charlie asked.

"It's like working with animals, stuff like that," Ack Ack answered.

"Boy, that'd be cool. You mean like a zoo keeper? Ole Penny would make some neat zoo keeper. She could hop right in there with the hippos and they'd think she was a long lost relative." Charlie got a mental picture of Penny and the hippos shaking hands and it took him several minutes to recover.

Ack Ack chortled gently. "She'd like that, oh, yes, she would," he said. "She'll have your scalp for that one, Charlie. The whole thing's too much for me." Ack Ack's face seemed to lengthen as Charlie watched. "I mean, that Ben thinks she's great. I just don't dig it. Captain Chubby herself. The old biological urge. It's too much."

Ack Ack and Charlie sat in silence, each thinking his own murky thoughts.

"What's up?" It was Arthur at the kitchen door.

"We were talking about Ben and Penny maybe getting married," Charlie said.

"Then you'd be related to each other," Arthur said firmly. "You'd be related by marriage. You'd have to have Christmas dinner together and give each other presents and all."

Charlie cracked his knuckles in despair.

"Quit that," Arthur said. He hated that noise. It sounded as if all the bones were being broken into tiny pieces and the fingers would be ruined forever. He would almost rather watch Charlie pick at a scab.

"You like white meat or dark?" Arthur asked Ack Ack.

"I don't even like turkey," Ack Ack said. "I am a picky eater."

"I like the second joint," Charlie said. "My father gets one second joint and I get the other."

"O.K., as long as Ack Ack doesn't care, that's good," Arthur said briskly. "How about stuffing? You've got to figure out what kind of stuffing everybody likes. My father makes ours and he puts celery and apple and onion and a mess of things in it. It's delicious."

"We have chestnuts in ours," Charlie said. Then he shouted, "What's all this garbage about stuffing and turkey? Ben's not going to get married. He's going to be a millionaire bachelor. He told me. And even if he does get married, he wouldn't marry *her* in a million years."

"Like I said," Ack Ack moved toward the door, "her bloodlines are of the finest. See you around. Tell Ben I was here."

Charlie and Arthur looked at each other. "You think he was sore?" Arthur asked.

"How do I know."

"Well, she's his sister, after all. Blood is thicker than water," Arthur said darkly.

"What's that mean?"

"I don't exactly know," Arthur admitted. "I think it means if somebody says something bad about a relative you've got to stick up for 'em."

"If Ben marries her," Charlie said, "I will never speak to him again as long as I live."

"They're not even through high school," Arthur said, "and they both have to go through college, so it'd be a long time off anyway."

"The Pig thinks she's so much. If she doesn't watch out, she's going to wear out that hair of hers. That is, if it isn't a wig already." Charlie laughed wildly. "The way she's always combing it and flipping it around! She's going to be bald if she doesn't watch it. She'll be some dish! She'll be some tomato when she turns up bald as a cue ball! What a gross out!"

"I don't know," Arthur said slowly, "she's not all that bad."

Charlie flexed his muscles. Then he started for the door.

"Where you going?" Arthur asked.

"Around," Charlie said. "Maybe to Ollie's. He's got a new spear gun. His father might take us snorkeling this summer. See you." And he started to run.

Arthur sat still for a couple of minutes. Then he went to the refrigerator and opened the door.

"Shut that!" Charlie's mother hollered. "I thought I told you . . ." She came into the kitchen. "Oh," she said, "I thought it was Charlie."

"My gosh," Arthur stammered, "I forgot where I was. I thought I was home." He backed toward the door. "Gosh," he said again, "I'm awful sorry. I didn't take anything. Honest."

He made his way down the back steps and out into the day. The street was empty. Arthur sat on the curb and threw pebbles at a spot of tar in the road, pretending it was a basket and the pebbles were the ball. He never missed. He was the star of the game. He could almost hear the crowds roaring in the stands.

t wasn't enough that Ben, finished fixing Mr. Acker-man's car, was now helping Captain Chubby write a term paper she was supposed to turn in after vacation. Oh no. That wasn't all, Charlie thought bitterly. Maybe blood really *was* thicker than water because the friendly feeling between Ack Ack and himself seemed to have cooled, plus his own brother, whom he shared a bathroom with and everything, wasn't speaking to him, and even Arthur hadn't been over lately. Everything was collapsing. As far as Charlie was concerned, Penny's vacation had lasted about a thousand years. She still had a week to go.

The thing that really tied it, that sent Charlie over the edge and made him realize drastic measures had to be taken, was when Ben spent his own dough to buy himself another white shirt and a pair of loafers, on account of Ed Reilly's mother said she wanted his loafers back pronto.

Ben was in bad shape. Something had to be done.

Charlie's friend Ollie gave him an idea. Ollie was an omnivorous reader. He read about things most kids had never heard of, like oceanography and stalactites and stalagmites and how to build an ice house to keep you warm if you felt like fishing through a hole in the ice in winter.

This week he was on a voodoo kick. "Listen to this," Ollie said. "This is really cool. You want to get rid of a toothache, you know what you do?" He peered over the edge of the page at Charlie.

"Sure, you go to the dentist and he loads you up with Novocain and yanks it out," Charlie answered.

"Your trouble is you got no imagination," Ollie said sternly. "What you do is you threaten the tooth with a new nail, then say 'Abracadabra' three times, make a cross on a mango tree, cut the cross off the tree, boil the bark. Wet the tooth with it and presto! no more toothache," he said, looking up from the book.

Using his fingers as a bookmark, Ollie smiled broadly. "Think of the money you'd save on dentist bills," he said.

"Great," Charlie said. "But what if you're fresh out of mango trees? That's something you didn't think of, I bet."

"That might present a problem," Ollie agreed, "but you could probably substitute maple or oak or one of those."

"What else does it tell you how to get rid of?" Charlie

asked. "I saw a movie once where this guy wanted to wipe out another guy and he made a doll that was supposed to be his enemy and he stuck pins in it and danced around it hollering all kinds of things and next thing you knew, the enemy was dead. It was pretty good."

"Hold it," Ollie commanded, "while I check. This book could be very useful." He flipped through some more pages.

"Here we are," he said. "It says if you want to get rid of somebody, you make a doll that's supposed to be the person you want to eliminate, stick it full of pins, and mix up a potion of a whole mess of stuff like garlic and leek and worm seed, whatever that is, add a shot of alcohol and have the person drink it. That person has got to be an awful sap to drink something like that," Ollie said reflectively. "Anyway, the book says after the person drinks the potion, he's had it. He gets a gigantic belly ache and dies. Any more questions you want answered?" Ollie asked. He looked terribly pleased with himself.

All Charlie wanted was to get rid of Captain Chubby. He didn't want to be quite that drastic, however. There was one thing about Ollie. He never went halfway.

"Done and done," Charlie said. "I gotta split." Ollie was too busy reading about how to call up spirits to pay any attention.

Outside, Charlie halfheartedly flexed his muscles. He sat on his front steps and thought black thoughts. He'd been thinking quite a few black thoughts lately. He watched Kathy, the little kid who lived across the street, beat up her baby doll and hurl it into its carriage.

Some mother you'll make, he thought sourly.

If he wasn't thinking black thoughts, he was thinking sour ones.

He was also in bad shape. Suddenly Charlie heard Ollie's voice describing the voodoo ritual to him, the sure way to eliminate an enemy. Make a Penny doll, stick it full of pins, and presto! no more Penny. Kathy had a doll. The coincidence stretched out its long arm and nudged him gently.

He crossed over and in a sweetsy-phony voice said, "Kathy, how about letting me borrow one of your old dolls?"

Kathy had a big gut on her for such a little kid, a lot of freckles, and a mean face.

"I love all my babies," she said. "I don't give them away. I take good care of them."

"Then how come you're giving that one a good going over?" Charlie asked. "Anyway, I only want to borrow one."

"That was just a tiny spanking," Kathy said.

"If that was a tiny spanking, I'd hate to see you give her a big one. You'd make some mother is all I can say."

Kathy stuck her tongue out at him and ran into her house. She was probably going to tell her mother a big story about him. She was that kind of a kid. She had a really lousy personality. She would probably be a lot like Penny when she grew up.

Charlie started for home. Then Kathy called, "You can have this one if you want. Her name's Mary." She held a limp object up for his inspection.

Mary had seen better days. She was pale gray. One eye was missing. She didn't have on any clothes. Charlie felt sorry for her.

"Hey, she's terrific! Great! Thanks a lot." He grabbed Mary by one leg and made for home. Mary would have to do. She was so far gone by now anyway, a few pins wouldn't make much difference.

When he reached his front door, he turned around. Kathy stood with her hands on her hips. She stuck her tongue out at him.

"You've got problems, kid," he yelled, and skinned inside before she demanded Mary back.

Charlie helped himself to his mother's plastic box of pins that she used for taking up hems and stuff like that. There were quite a few, enough to do a thorough job. He closed the door to his room, stuck pins all over Mary's decrepit body, a few in her head for good measure, all the while avoiding her one good eye. There was something about it that made him feel guilty. It stared at him, blue and glassy. Why did dolls always have blue eyes? Charlie covered the eye carefully with one hand while he finished.

"The hex is on," he said from between tight lips. "The voodoo is at work. Begone, get lost, take off." These may not have been the actual words used by ancient practitioners of voodoo but they would have to do. Charlie stuffed her under his mattress to wait for things to take hold.

"Who are you talking to?" his mother asked. She had a habit of popping up at inconvenient times.

"I'm talking to myself," Charlie said hastily.

"That means one of two things. Either you've got money in the bank or you're losing your marbles," Charlie's mother said. She had a big supply of old wives' tales at her fingertips. "And I know you don't have any money, so I must draw my own conclusions."

"Ha, ha," Charlie said sarcastically.

He had a rough time getting to sleep that night. It must've been close to midnight before he realized that Mary made quite a lump in the mattress. He fumbled in the dark and dragged her out and threw her on the floor until morning.

C an you get the car for tomorrow night?" Ack Ack asked Ben. His motorbike was no good for taking girls out on dates and Ack Ack and Ben were doubling tomorrow night. He had discovered that when parents of girls he dated looked out the window and saw his bike, they invariably said, "Nothing doing," or "You're not riding on *that* thing!"

Ack Ack had long ago got over hurt feelings he might have had from derogatory remarks cast against his pride and joy. He didn't realize that part of the adults' reaction was based on his appearance. His enormous helmet and whispery voice and his habit of looking over his shoulder to see if he was being trailed did nothing to reassure them that here was a young man whom they could trust.

And his mustache didn't help. That mustache was finally beginning to look like one. It represented a lot of work.

Ben rolled a cigarette.

"The old man gives me the what-have-you-done-for-me-lately routine," Ben said, "and when I reminded him that I had washed and waxed the car—on my day off yet—he was backed into a corner. He said I could have it for tomorrow but that if I left the gas tank empty it would be the last time I'd get it for about a hundred years. He really gets clutched because a couple of times he's run out of gas on his way to the station to catch his train. So you'll have to kick in with a buck for gas."

"Right on," Ack Ack nodded sagely. "I've got the same kind of old man."

"What are you guys going to see?" Charlie asked.

"We're going to the Capitol to see the Beefeaters do a concert."

"Those the guys who eat raw hamburger while they play?" Charlie wanted to know.

"Yeah. They're cool," Ben said. "The big guy, the one who plays the bass guitar, they say he eats about five pounds of meat during one concert."

"How much do the tickets cost?" Ack Ack looked worried. A motorbike was an expensive proposition. He had a big bill at the garage for repairs.

"Only two and a half apiece," Ben said.

" 'Only' he says," Ack Ack hollered. "Only! You think I'm made of money?"

"Who you taking? Cora?"

Ack Ack looked mournful. "Last time I had a date with Cora, her mother and father said 'groovy' and 'outasight' and stuff like that. It was pretty embarrassing. Her old man wanted a ride on my bike and everything. I don't know why people their age don't act their age. They ought to know better," Ack Ack said sternly. "Besides, Cora's pre-engaged to Neil Carey. They've been going steady since Tuesday. You're taking Penny, right?"

"Who else?" Charlie said. If he'd been smart, he would've kept his trap shut. He liked to sit in a corner and listen to Ben and Ack Ack rapping. He figured he learned a lot about life that way. It was best not to call attention to himself.

Ben shot him a look and said, "Little pitchers have big ears," which always burned Charlie up.

"Penny feel all right?" Charlie asked Ack Ack. He didn't put too much faith in this voodoo bit. He remembered that when he was just a kid, like seven or eight, he tried it on a teacher who hated him and whom he also hated and it hadn't worked then. Now he'd try anything.

"Far as I know," Ack Ack said. "Why?"

"I thought I heard somebody say she didn't feel good," Charlie said hastily.

"Why not try Laurie?" Ben asked.

"Laurie who?"

"The one with her own Mustang. I think her last name's Roache or Bugg or something like that."

"What do you mean, something like that? Something little that crawls? How about Ant or Gnat? Or Cater-

pillar? That would be a good last name, Caterpillar."
Ack Ack wheezed his amusement.

"She lives on Magruder Drive, I think. She gave me
a ride home last week and, man, that car's outasight!"

"You think she would let me use her car if I asked
her out?" Ack Ack asked. "I've never driven a Mustang."

"Not the first go round," Ben cautioned. "Better wait
until you ask her out a second time to ask her if you
can drive it. She might get suspicious otherwise."

"What does she look like?" Ack Ack asked. "I can't
get a picture of her in my mind."

"She's sort of tall with sort of brownish hair and an
O.K. build and she has quite a few teeth and she laughs
a lot."

"That must be the one who sits in back of me in
biology class," Ack Ack said. "Either that or it's her twin
sister. I wish she sat beside me," he said wistfully.

"Why?" Charlie asked.

"Because she gets practically straight A's and if she
sat next to me I could slide the old eyeballs over to her
paper every once in a while and pick up some pointers
and then I too might get straight A's in biology."

"You'd stoop to that?" Ben asked.

"I think so," Ack Ack admitted. He had been having
a very rough year in biology. "I would like to think
I could resist temptation but I am basically a very
weak individual," he said.

"So call her now. Why do you always wait until the
last minute?"

"I don't like to plan ahead," Ack Ack explained unnecessarily. "I never know what might come up at the last minute and I like to hold my time open in case something spectacular should show."

"Like what?"

Ack Ack looked vague, which he did with surpassing skill. "Who knows? Think big. Maybe a trip around the world or an offer to go on safari in Africa. Or maybe I'll win the lottery and take off for California to surf. If I win the lottery I am going to buy myself the most expensive surfboard I can find and maybe go to Australia and Hawaii after California. I might never come back," Ack Ack said.

"In the meantime," Ben said, "call Laurie." He was used to hearing what Ack Ack planned to do when he hit the big time.

Ack Ack dialed the number he found in the phone book. Laurie's last name turned out to be Roache after all.

"Hello," he said, putting his hand around the receiver and peering into the corners of the room to make sure he wasn't being eavesdropped upon. "Is Laurie there?

"Oh, this *is* Laurie. This is Ack Ack Ackerman. I just happen to have two tickets for a concert tomorrow at the Capitol featuring the Beefeaters and I wonder if you could go. . . . Yeah, I'll wait."

He put his hand over the receiver. "She went to ask her mother," he whispered.

"Oh, is her mother going too? That'll make for a pretty full car," Ben said.

Ack Ack paled. "I can't afford three tickets," he said. Say what you would about Ack Ack, he was a great guy but a little on the slow side at times.

He hung up after more conversation.

"She can go," he said gloomily. "She didn't say anything about using her Mustang, though."

"We lead into that nice and easy," Ben said. "I'll put on my good-luck hat and psych Laurie into lending us her Mustang. Never fear."

Mary swung lightly to and fro in the breeze. The pins had proved worthless. Penny was in as good health as ever so Charlie had rigged Mary up on his ceiling-light cord in an intricate noose arrangement.

"What am I doing wrong?" Charlie asked himself out loud. "I must have left something out."

He patted Mary's pin-dotted stomach.

"It's not your fault, kid," he said. Mary, whose ghostly presence had become so familiar that Charlie would have missed her if she had not been there, stared stonily at him with her eye. She didn't answer.

"What on earth is that?" Charlie's mother asked.

Charlie jumped.

"How come you're always creeping around?" he felt like saying but didn't. Charlie's mother wore sneakers most of the time and they gave her a decided advantage. She could and did come up on him unexpectedly, whereas if she wore shoes, like most people's mothers, he would have plenty of warning. She didn't even play tennis.

"I'm just practicing my boy-scout knots, Ma," he said. He couldn't very well say, "I'm putting the hex on Penny the Pig and in case the pins don't work, I'm cutting off the supply of oxygen to the brain."

Some brain.

"That seems a peculiar way to practice them," his mother said. Then she said, "Don't call me 'Ma,' " as he had known she would. That always served as a diversion. Any time Charlie wanted to sidetrack her from a subject that might prove embarrassing, he called her "Ma." She hated it.

"How come you wear sneakers when you don't even play tennis?" Charlie asked.

She smiled. "Because I like to sneak around," she answered, confirming his suspicions. "Get it? Sneak around in sneakers?"

She looked at him expectantly, waiting for the laugh. She was the kind of mother who really liked her own jokes. If you wanted to get on the good side of her, just laugh at a few of them.

"I get it," Charlie said, "but notice I am not rolling on the floor."

"If you did, you'd suffocate once those dust balls got to you," she said. "I thought you were supposed to have cleaned under the bed last Saturday."

"I forgot," Charlie said.

"Where is Ben?" she asked.

"Over at the Pig's house, where else?"

"Over at whose house?" she raised her eyebrows.

"Penny's. Ack Ack says his father's going to start charging Ben room and board, he spends so much time there."

"I hope he's not planning on charging him more than about fifty cents a week because that's about all he could afford," she said.

"Do *you* like her, Mom?"

"Like who?"

"You know who. Penny. Ack Ack's sister Penny."

"Oh, her. I don't really know her. How could I like or not like her?" his mother asked.

"If you got to know her, you'd really hate her," Charlie said.

"If Ben likes her, she can't be all bad," his mother said.

"Oh, yeah?" Charlie said. "That's what *you* think."

"And I'll tell you something else. Arthur says if they get married we'll have to have Christmas dinner together on account of we'll be relatives and they have their turkey stuffed with a bunch of junk and they don't like the second joint," Charlie finished.

Charlie's mother looked dazed. "Listen," she said. Then "Never mind. I'll have to go and think this one through."

She sneaked away on her sneakers. Charlie and Mary watched her go.

Is Ben there?"

It was Ack Ack.

"No, he's still at work. What do you want, Ack Ack?" Charlie asked.

"How'd you know it was me?" Ack Ack asked, surprised.

"Oh, I don't know. I just did."

"Well, tell him I want to know if he thinks we have to take these cats out and tie on the old feed bag after the concert. Tell him after I get through paying for the tickets, I'm practically out of bread. Tell him I thought maybe we could just say 'So long, girls,' kiss them good night, and then toss 'em out of the car in front of their houses and take off."

"Listen," Charlie said, "if it was me, I wouldn't spend a plugged nickel on either one of 'em."

"I know the feeling well," Ack Ack whispered confidentially into the phone, "so that's all right, boy. Just take my word for it, though, Charlie, things will change. I remember when I too was a broth of a boy and the opposite sex was a blot on the escutcheon. But times change, Charlie, and you will find that the girls grow up to be beauteous creatures that have a definite appeal. It is too bad, in my opinion, that they are so expensive. I myself see nothing wrong in the great old American custom of the dutch treat, but I have been unsuccessful so far in my attempts at selling it."

"What's 'dutch treat' mean?" Charlie asked. Even if half of Ack Ack's conversation went over his head, he enjoyed listening to him and being treated as an equal.

"That's when you have the pleasure of the lady's company and all, but she pays her own way. For everything. Food, drink, movies, concerts, and taxi fare. Or bus fare, if that's the kind of guy you are. Sort of a women's lib routine. It's the only way to go," Ack Ack concluded.

"It sounds like a good idea to me too," Charlie agreed. "If I ever ask a girl out anywhere, which I probably won't, I think I might tell her it's dutch treat or no soap."

"You are a smart boy, my friend," Ack Ack said. "Far smarter than I or your brother or anybody I know, for that matter. Start off on the right foot and you've got it made. Treat 'em rough and they love it. Did you ever see that Jimmy Cagney movie where he pushes this grapefruit in this girl's face and she loves it? Did you see that one?"

"No," Charlie said. "I know I would remember that if I saw it. That's one I missed."

"Next time I see it scheduled on the late late show I will advise you of same. It is one of the great ones."

"That'd be cool," Charlie said.

"O.K., sport, now tell Ben I called and tell him what I want answered. You have to decide these things in advance. That way you can be sure there's no slip up."

"Right on," Charlie said, borrowing one of Ack Ack's favorite phrases. "Done and done. I'll see he gets the message."

"I'm splitting," Ack Ack whispered and hung up.

Sammy, this is my friend Arthur. The one who makes up poetry," Charlie said. "Arthur, meet Sammy."

"Pleased to make your acquaintance, Arthur," Sammy said. "You'd be about a size sixteen, with a thirteen and a half neck, I would guess." Sammy always liked to make sure which size a person was before he got down to conversation. "I got a very nice three-piece suit here that might be just the thing for you. I happen to personally know that the party I purchased it from has all his garments custom-made. It is a lovely piece of cloth. A Harris tweed."

"Three pieces?" Arthur said.

"That's the coat, the pants, and the vest. A vest is a must for the well-dressed man. Not to mention it keeps the drafts off the chest and so cuts down on pulmonary infection," Sammy said.

The tomcat surveyed Arthur and Charlie scornfully.

"How's Ben?" Sammy asked. "He still got the same lady friend?"

"Yeah," Charlie said. "I'm afraid so."

"A fine young lady, I am sure," he said. "Would you like to have a look at a new shipment of merchandise I just got in? A couple of nice sport coats, a Norfolk jacket that's a beauty, and a tie or two that might hit the spot."

"How are you fixed for hats, Sammy?" Charlie asked. "What I would really like is a black hat like Ben's, the one like Humphrey Bogart wore."

"Ah, Mr. Bogart," Sammy said fondly. "All the customers want a hat like Mr. Bogart's. They are not easy to come by. A genuine Humphrey Bogart number is a very rare bird, you might say. Not only do you have trouble finding the hats, you have trouble fitting them to the proper person. Not everyone is the type. The hat is no good on the wrong head."

"You mean if it doesn't fit?" Charlie asked.

"I mean it's a question of *joie de vivre*," Sammy said.

Arthur and Charlie both looked as if they had been struck on the head with a blunt instrument.

"That's French," Sammy explained, not without pride. "It means you ought to have a joy of living, of life, the way Mr. Bogart and those of his ilk did in order to wear a Bogart-styled hat with aplomb. Ben has got the *joie de vivre* and the aplomb. Maybe you boys will have it, too, in a couple of years."

"Ben calls it his good-luck hat," Charlie said.

Sammy nodded approvingly. "That's about it," he said. "When he has got that hat on his head, there is nothing he cannot do. It is a state of mind."

"He doesn't wear it that much any more," Charlie said. "Penny, this girl he likes, doesn't go in for that kind of stuff. I've asked him a hundred times if I can have it but he won't give it to me. He's a regular dog in the manger."

"He may get back to it," Sammy said. "Give him time. I can see his reasons. Even if he doesn't wear it, he knows it's there. Now how about a spot of poetry?"

Sammy was prepared. He propped an enormously fat book up on a table cluttered with old clothes. "Sit yourselves down," Sammy said. "Any place you can find." He scooped more old clothes off the seat of a dilapidated sofa. "Make yourselves cozy," he said.

Charlie had told Arthur about what a character Sammy was, about his crossed eyes and the way he liked to size everybody up before he got involved in conversation.

"Ben says he is one of nature's noblemen," Charlie had said as he and Arthur walked to Sammy's, "and I think he is right. He will give you the shirt off his back if he likes you. He is his own boss and he is an honest man, as he will probably tell you. I like to listen to Sammy. He says a lot of stuff you really have to think about. He didn't go to college, but he is a heck of a lot smarter than lots of guys who did, I bet."

"We will start with 'Paul Revere's Ride' by Mr. Henry

Wadsworth Longfellow," Sammy said now that they were settled. "I want you to listen to the story it tells. It is about an event that actually happened, which no one can deny."

Sammy started off: " 'Listen, my children, and you shall hear/Of the midnight ride of Paul Revere.' " And whether it was the way he really got carried away with the poem and his face got red and his eyes bounced around something fierce, or the way his voice rose and fell for dramatic effect, Charlie did not know, but he and Arthur were spellbound.

When Sammy got to the part where Paul Revere springs to his saddle, "But lingers and gazes, till full on his sight/A second lamp in the belfry burns!" all three of them were ready to cheer.

"You would make a neat teacher," Charlie said as Sammy wiped his brow. "You would really grab the kids' attention."

Arthur said, "That old Paul Revere was some gutsy guy, right?" and Sammy nodded agreement.

"Next time I'll try a little of Lochinvar on you two. Not the whole thing at once, it's too long, just a little." Sammy looked serious. "We don't want to run Lochinvar into the ground before you get the feel of it."

The bell tinkled and a couple of middle-aged ladies came into the store.

"Excuse me, boys, don't go away," Sammy said. "I will tend to the customers and be right back."

Charlie and Arthur pressed back into the depths of

the sofa and the old clothes and listened as one of the ladies explained that she and her husband had been invited to a costume party to which they were to come dressed as characters in an old movie.

"So I got this darling idea," the lady said, "and I thought my husband and I could go as Fred Astaire and Ginger Rogers. I have this dreamy dress with feathers and all that I got from my mother-in-law, and it's straight out of one of Ginger's movies, and I thought if you had a tail coat and maybe a top hat, why, my husband, he's a divine dancer anyway, he could be Fred Astaire."

There was a silence and Charlie could hear the tom-cat making noises of displeasure in his throat.

Finally, Sammy said, "I do not happen to have anything of that description at the moment. I am sorry."

"Oh dear," the lady said. "I was counting on you."

"I bet you got plenty of dough for that coat and hat that Ben wanted, didn't you, Sammy?" Charlie asked when the ladies had left.

Sammy scratched his head.

"I didn't sell it yet," he said. "I still got it in the back room."

"Oh," Charlie said. "Then how come you didn't sell it to her?" and he gestured to the door.

"I keep thinking Ben might change his mind," Sammy said. "Who knows? We all change our minds now and then. It is good for a person to change his mind. It keeps him flexible."

"Sammy," Charlie said, "you lied to the lady. You said you didn't have a top hat and tail coat. I thought you were an honest man."

Sammy's eyes came together over the bridge of his nose and he smiled. He didn't look at all ashamed. "I am," he said. "I am a very honest man. But we all got to have our little lapses here and there. Now I'll get out the saltines and put the kettle on. And Arthur, I would be honored if you would read me a poem or two of your own making."

Arthur pulled out the big envelope he had stuffed under his sweater.

"I just happen to have a couple of them with me," he said.

ck Ack was uptight. You could tell even before
he came in, sat down, and started biting his
fingernails. Usually, he said "Ciao," took out the
cigarette he kept behind his ear, lipped it around for
a couple of minutes, put it back, hitched his pants
legs up and started in on a long, philosophical dis-
cussion.

Charlie's and Ben's mother enjoyed Ack Ack. He
made her feel very sophisticated, she said. Their father
said, "I have my doubts about that kid," and Ben said,
"He's all right. He may seem a little peculiar once in a
while but he's true blue. You shouldn't judge a person
by his appearance."

The night of the concert Ack Ack wore a modish
pair of plaid trousers, topped off by a green shirt with
no sleeves, like the top of an old-fashioned men's bath-

ing suit. He had an ascot around his neck and wore no shoes.

He admired himself in the hall mirror.

"That's class," he murmured. His mustache had grown some and he looked more woebegone and pursued than last week.

"My mother's blowing her brains out about this," he said, stroking the mustache. "My father says he gives me two days to shave it off, and if I don't he's going to sit on my head and do the job himself."

"Will he?" Charlie asked.

Ack Ack shrugged. "Probably. It gives him a feeling of power to be able to direct my actions to the point where he acts as my barber. If the guy wants to, well, he can shave it off. It is important in his projection of his idea of himself that I be clean shaven. It is a sort of status thing for a guy his age to have a son with no facial hair. He probably raps about it all the time with his peers on the train. The funny thing is, I've seen some of those cats when they hop off that old choo-choo and a lot of them have burns and beards and the works. Boy, do they ever look raunchy!"

Charlie blinked. "Half the time I don't know what you're talking about, Ack Ack," he said.

"That's all right, kid." Ben came in. "He doesn't know what he's talking about either, so that makes two of you."

Ack Ack paced back and forth. "Let's split," he said.

"Keep your hair on," Ben said, combing his own carefully, polishing his loafers with a dirty undershirt. He wore a white shirt, a pair of flannels, and socks with his loafers.

"You're not going like that?" Ack Ack asked. "You've got to be out of your mind."

It was the socks that got to him.

"You're going to a concert dressed like that?"

Charlie thought that Ack Ack would probably be ashamed to be seen with Ben.

"You do your thing, buddy, and I'll do mine," Ben said, and tilted his good-luck hat off the bedpost.

"All right, sweetheart, let's go," he said and all of a sudden he was Humphrey Bogart. "Suave," he said, "very suave."

"Square," Ack Ack said, "very square. How come you let some chick change your whole life-style? Especially some chick like my baby sister?" He shook his head in bewilderment.

Charlie felt like kissing Ack Ack for saying that. Ack Ack had hit the nail on the head. Maybe Ben would listen to him.

"Whose life-style?" Ben asked. "Not mine. I maintain my individuality; you look like everybody else. Ever think of that?"

"I'm getting nervous," Ack Ack said, unnecessarily. "How do I know this Laurie and I will be compatible? I wonder if it's worth it."

"If what's worth what?" Charlie asked.

"This Mustang. I would just like to get my mitts on it

for one brief moment. Get the picture," and Ack Ack closed his eyes and smiled dreamily, "of me blasting around town behind the wheel of a Mustang."

"All right, kid, I'm ready. Let's get out of here," Ben said.

"What time will you be home, Ben?" his father asked, giving him the car keys.

"Well," Ben said evasively, "the concert's over at eleven and then we have to take the girls out to feed them."

Ack Ack looked pained.

"I thought we decided against that," he said. "I'm low on bread. I told Charlie to tell you."

"You can spring for a hamburger and french fries. Do you want Laurie to think you're a cheapskate?" Ben asked.

"Why not? I am," Ack Ack said simply. "I don't want to start off under false pretenses. This chick better get the picture right off."

"Why not go to one of those cheap hamburger joints?" Ben's father asked. "What do they cost, ten, fifteen cents? And that includes the ketchup and bun. Surely the girls are worth fifteen cents."

Ack Ack started to explain why this might not be the case and Ben had to drag him out, still talking, still waving his hands.

"Your old man is a very understanding guy, for a father," Ack Ack told Ben.

"Other people's fathers are always more understanding than your own," Ben commented and, with a great roaring of engine and blowing of horn, he prepared for take-off.

"Don't forget those seat belts," Ben's mother shouted.

"Your mother's hollering at you," Ack Ack said, looking back at the house.

"I know," Ben answered. "She always does. Mostly she does when Charlie's in the car, but I guess she feels responsible for you too."

Ack Ack considered this piece of information. "Why does she do that? Do you listen to her?"

"Sure I listen. I usually smile and wave at her and that makes her feel better. She ought to make a recording and just open the kitchen window and play it every time I drive away."

"Does she always holler the same thing?"

"Yeah."

"What does she say?"

"She says 'Don't forget to fasten your seat belts' or a variation of that."

Ack Ack rolled down the window. He listened for a minute. "You're right," he said. "Why don't we let the girls sit in back and we'll strap ourselves in up front, just so's your mother'll feel better?"

"No," Ben said. "You and Laurie sit in back. You want to drive that Mustang or not?"

"Oh, I do, I do," Ack Ack said earnestly. "Hey, slow down, there's Charlie."

Charlie was out of breath.

"Mom says to be sure and fasten your seat belts," he said.

"I know, we are," Ben said.

"I was just suggesting to Ben that we strap ourselves in front and let the ladies sit in back," Ack Ack said.

"Hey, Ack Ack, try to pretend you're chivalrous, even if you're not," Ben pleaded.

"You know something?" Ack Ack asked. "I don't think chivalry is my bag."

ow was it?" Charlie asked. He had tried to stay awake until Ben got home from the concert, but he must've dropped off because the next thing he knew it was morning.

"How was what?" Ben sounded surly. He lay in bed with his arm over his eyes. Suddenly he sat up, took his Bogie hat from the bedpost, and threw it into the wastebasket.

"And who says you can just come charging in here without knocking or anything?" he demanded.

"How was the concert?" Charlie asked again. "The Beefeaters. Hey, don't do that. What're you doing?"

"What's it look like I'm doing? I'm throwing that lousy old hat away, that's what." Ben got out of bed, put his foot in the basket, and stomped everything down as far as it would go.

"Give it to me if you don't want it," Charlie yelped. "I love that hat. Give it to me."

"It's no good," Ben said savagely. "It's just a lousy old hat that looks like it has been caught in a hurricane. Forget it." He got back into bed and turned his face to the wall.

"What the heck's the matter with you? You're some nice guy to have around the house these days. You're some . . ."

"Just don't bug me. Mind your own business. All you and Mom do is bug me. Just don't talk to me, all right?"

Charlie went outside and sat on the front stoop. It was Sunday. Sunday could be very depressing. What the heck. Falling for some stupid bossy girl sure didn't improve anyone's disposition. Look at Ben. Always before he'd been easygoing, laughing, a really nice guy. A friend. Look at him now.

Kathy from across the street saw Charlie and yelled, "Hey, I want Mary back."

Charlie zoomed back inside, pretending he hadn't heard her, although he would've had to be stone deaf not to. The kid had a voice on her like a foghorn.

It was getting so that even the front stoop was a dangerous spot. Maybe if he snuck out the back door he could get to Arthur's without anyone's stopping him.

"Did you empty the garbage?" his mother asked as he scuttled through the kitchen.

"Sure Mom." From where he was he could see coffee grounds and eggshells pushing the top of the garbage pail into a standing position.

"Have you done your homework?" she asked as he started to empty the garbage.

"Mom, it's Sunday morning." He spilled coffee grounds in a tiny trail behind him.

Escape, escape.

"Charlie, would you mind riding your bike down to get the papers? Your father's still asleep and I'm not dressed," she said.

Right on. A ride in the open air would be a relief.

As Charlie was stopped at a light, a black Porsche pulled alongside him. He looked at it, thinking, Boy, what I wouldn't give for a boat like that. A girl's voice said, "Good morning, Charlie. How are you, dear boy?"

It was Penny. Sitting in the Porsche. Charlie's mouth dropped open. He stared. He couldn't help it, he just stared.

The Porsche and Charlie both pulled up outside the paper store, which saved a lot of time because Charlie had planned to follow them anyway.

"Charlie, this is Robby Barnes," Penny said. She had never sounded friendlier, more sweetsy and phony. "Robby, this is Ben's brother, Charlie."

Those must be some bar bells this guy uses, Charlie thought as he shook hands. Wow. This Robby Barnes had a handshake like a pro-football player. He wasn't any taller than Ben but he was about twice as wide. His neck must've measured eighteen inches, Charlie figured, just the way Sammy would've. And even though he wore a tweed jacket, Charlie fancied he could see the muscles rippling underneath.

"That's some car," Charlie said.

"Isn't it?" Penny smiled. "Robby wanted to drive to

the concert last night but Ben insisted he drive. And anyway there isn't room for more than two in a Porsche."

"He went too?" Charlie asked.

"Robby goes to school near where I do. He stopped by yesterday to ask if I wanted a ride back today, so I talked him into staying and going with us," Penny said, putting her arm through Robby's.

"How'd you like it?"

"Well, I've seen a lot of really fantastic groups play," Robby said, "but I guess if you've never seen any of them, any of the really big ones, they were all right. A little bit amateurish, but they'll probably shape up with experience."

"That's what I thought too," Penny said.

"I heard they were supposed to be great," Charlie said. "How about the guy who eats all the hamburger while he plays?"

"He was out sick," Penny said. "Would you like a ride in Robby's Porsche, Charlie? It's fantastic. I bet you've never ridden in one before."

"I bet you never have either," Charlie said. Behind Robby's back, Penny narrowed her eyes and drew her finger across her throat in a slitting motion. She did not look friendly.

"No thanks," Charlie said. "I've got to get the papers back before my father wakes up."

He watched them drive away. He would've given anything for a ride in that buggy. But not with El Piggo and Mr. Muscles at the wheel.

he telephone was ringing as Charlie came in the door. It was Ack Ack.

"Hey, sport, let me speak to Ben."

"He's still in bed, Ack Ack. I don't think he feels too good."

"That I can understand. Just give him a message. Tell him I think if I hop on my bike and retrace our route, I might possibly be able to case the spot where the bill blew out the window. With any luck at all, I can find it and, if I do, I'll take half."

"What bill?"

"He didn't tell you? Well, this cat Robby, he offered to pay, he insisted on paying for everybody's burgers when we went to eat after the concert, and Ben was sore, see, and I don't blame him. He wasn't going to let that guy pay for him and Penny, and he took two bucks out of his wallet and threw them at Robby, then he drove away so fast one of the bills blew out the window.

I almost jumped out to rescue it but when I got a look at the speedometer, I decided against it. I mean, I might've broken an arm or a leg, right? I'm not chicken but I just sat there and watched that bill float away. Now I think I might find it."

"How come this Robby guy went along?" Charlie asked.

"Penny asked Ben if he minded and what could he say? Of course he minded. She is such a stinker. Robby wanted to pay for a tank of gas and Ben turned him down. Wow. Sometimes I just don't dig that brother of yours. A free tank of gas and he says Nyet."

"How was Laurie?" Charlie asked. "How'd you like her?"

"She's some cool chick. She's a nice kid, knows a lot about music. She's in my biology class, you know? So I decided to give biology a whirl, just for starters. So I give the reproductive system of plants a try, on account of that's what we just covered in class. And you know what? Next thing I know I'm describing to Laurie the reproductive system of humans. I tell you, it was pretty hairy there for a minute."

Charlie could practically see Ack Ack wiping his forehead.

"My father's yelling at me," Ack Ack said. "I've got to go. He wants to go to work on my mustache. I gotta beat him to the punch."

"What are you going to do?" Charlie could hear Ack Ack's father in the background.

"I'm going to shave it off myself. I never really liked it that much to start with. I just grew it to antagonize the old man. Now that I've accomplished my objective, all right. I gotta split, chief. Tell Ben I called. Tell him about the bill."

"O.K.," Charlie said.

"Yeh, yeh," Ack Ack whispered, and was gone.

The hat was still in Ben's wastebasket. Charlie took it out, brushed it off, and tried it on.

"All right, sweetheart," he lisped, "cut the comedy and tell me where you hid the swag." Humphrey Bogart to a T. "You fool, you," Charlie whispered. He was Peter Lorre. Peter Lorre always said that. Charlie figured that he and Lorre were about the same size too, Lorre being an undersized guy.

What did Lorre say besides "You fool, you?" Charlie had seen *The Maltese Falcon* about five times on television. The last time, he'd set the alarm for two A.M. when the movie began and then he fell asleep in his father's chair before it ended, and woke up in the morning just before his mother came down to start breakfast. That was a close one.

"You blundering fathead," Charlie whispered. He popped his eyeballs out and pulled the hat down at a sinister angle. That was what Lorre called Sidney Green-street. Arthur would make a good Sidney Greenstreet. *They* were about the same size.

"You blundering fathead," he said again. He wished he'd thought to call Penny that this morning.

Charlie put Ben's hat in his bureau drawer, next to Mary. If Ben didn't want it, he, Charlie, did. He'd decided to collect hats. Some kids collected baseball cards, some old bottles or hubcaps. He'd much rather be a hat collector.

Downstairs, his father was playing solitaire and watching a ball game on TV. His mother was taking down the dining-room curtains, clucking about how filthy they were.

"How come you're doing that on Sunday?" Charlie asked her.

"Because by Monday I won't have the strength," she said.

Ben came in from the B and T where he worked on Sundays until four. He went to his room without speaking.

"All right, where is it?" He came storming out.

"Where's what?" Charlie asked, knowing.

"My hat. The hat in the wastebasket. I put it there and some wise guy took it. Whoever it was, he's got exactly three seconds to give it back." Ben's face was tight with anger.

"You threw it away," Charlie said. "You said you didn't want it."

"I changed my mind."

"Suppose Mom had thrown it in the garbage and the garbage men came to collect it. What then?"

"She didn't and they didn't and let's have it."

Charlie grumbled all the way to his dresser. "Next time you throw something in the wastebasket and I take it out, it's mine," he said. "For keeps."

"Dream on," Ben said.

"I saw Penny this morning," Charlie said. Suddenly he wanted to hurt Ben. "She was with this muscle-bound character in a Porsche. That is some car. Outasight!"

Ben didn't answer. He started up the stairs.

"She's going back to school today," Charlie said.

Ben came back down part way.

"No she's not," he said. "She's not going back until Tuesday. She has to finish her term paper."

"She told me he was driving her back today. I guess she's going to finish her paper back there."

"I don't believe you," Ben said flatly.

"O.K., so don't. Call up and find out for yourself. Why would I make up a story like that?"

"Get out of here, you little creep," Ben yelled. "I've got work to do."

He slammed around his room for a while. Charlie didn't hear him go to the phone. He sat and looked at his spelling homework and wrote down *their* and *there* and *they're* and decided maybe he'd learn Russian instead of English. It couldn't be anywhere near as hard.

"Supper's ready, boys." They all sat down. Their father asked Ben how the concert had been.

"I've seen better," he said shortly.

"I almost forgot," Charlie said. "Ack Ack called and said to tell you he thinks he can find the dollar bill if he goes back on his bike to where it blew out of the car."

"What dollar bill?" Charlie's mother asked.

"I don't know why no one can have any privacy around here," Ben said. "May I be excused?"

"Let him go," his mother said to his father.

"What's eating him?" he wanted to know.

Ben thundered up the stairs.

"A disease called youth," she said.

"It's not eating me," Charlie said, taking a second helping, "and I'm young."

"It will," she said. "Give it time."

A week passed, a week during which Ben hardly spoke to anyone. He came home, checked the hall table where the day's mail was placed, thrashed through the pile a couple of times, then went to his room, closed the door, and didn't come out until suppertime.

Charlie's father said, "If that kid's manners don't improve, there's going to be trouble. I'm not running a hotel, and he better understand it."

"I'm afraid he's been rejected," his mother said. "Rejection always comes hard."

Charlie had quite a time looking up *rejection* in the dictionary because he spelled it with a *g* instead of a *j*. He finally got it right and found out that it meant "refuse to accept" or "discard" or "throw away." So what's that mean? he asked himself. Ben had been discarded?

Charlie thought about that for a while. Only yesterday he'd heard Ack Ack ask Ben if he'd heard from Penny yet.

"Not yet," Ben had said in an offhand voice. "She must be pretty busy, getting back after vacation and all. Did your mother and father hear from her?"

"Well, she called collect when she got there. They always tell her to call collect, like she was going across the country in a covered wagon and they want to be sure the Indians didn't get her. Chee."

Then this morning Charlie was going through the trash to see if he could find the hunting knife he'd borrowed from Ollie which was missing now that Ollie wanted it back. He didn't find the knife but he came upon wads of paper which, on inspection, proved to be unfinished letters, starting "Dear Penny, I have been thinking of you . . ." or "Dear Penny, Things are really hopping around here. Today . . ."

Charlie was no dope. No matter what kind of marks he got in school, he could put two and two together as well as the next guy.

So Captain Chubby had rejected Ben in favor of Mr. Muscles and his Flying Porsche. She was a bigger fink than even Charlie had thought. He felt like writing her a letter telling her that. As a matter of fact, if letters didn't need an eight-cent stamp, he would've.

But she wasn't worth eight cents. Not in Charlie's book.

Charlie had just barely put his thumb out when the red Mustang pulled up and stopped.

"You want a lift?" the girl said.

"Hey," Charlie said, sinking into the upholstery, "it smells new."

"It is," she said. "I got it for my birthday."

"Is your name Laurie?" Charlie asked. He had just put two and two together again.

"How did you know?" the girl said, smiling at him. She drove pretty slow and in the middle of the road. She also stopped at every intersection and practically got out of the car to see if there was anything coming. Charlie figured she hadn't been driving too long.

"I'm Ben's brother," Charlie said.

She smiled even more.

"That's a cool hat," Charlie said. "Did you get it at Sammy's?" Laurie's hat was purple with yellow flowers and a big floppy brim. It looked like a Sammy special.

"What's Sammy's?" she asked.

"It's this place Ben buys a lot of stuff at," Charlie said and before he knew it he was telling Laurie about his Sherlock Holmes job and his muffler and the tail coat. Laurie was a very easy girl to talk to.

Charlie was pleased that Ack Ack and Ben were in front of the house when Laurie's Mustang pulled up. He especially liked the way Ack Ack's mouth dropped open.

"Where'd you find him?" Ben asked Laurie.

"He was hitching a ride and I picked him up," she explained.

"Don't you know it's dangerous to pick up hitch-hikers?" he asked.

Laurie shrugged. "I figured he was small enough so I could handle him," she said. "And anyway, he looked like a good kid. Also," she said offhandedly, "I know some karate and if he got out of line I could take care of him."

"Where'd you learn karate?" Charlie wanted to know. He was impressed.

"From my father. He has a brown belt," she said.

"I like that hat," Ben said. "Did you get that at Sammy's?"

"No, I've never been there. Charlie asked me that too. He said he'd take me there some time."

"She's cool," Charlie said after Laurie had left. "And you know what? She's going to let me drive her Mustang."

"When?" Ack Ack yelped. "You are a mere babe in swaddling clothes."

"When I get my driver's license. She said I could when I get my license."

"I don't think that's such a hot idea," Ack Ack said. "That's a very powerful car. You might go through the garage wall, like Penny almost did."

"He wouldn't do a thing as stupid as that," Ben said. "That's something only a girl would pull."

"Not a girl like Laurie," Charlie said. "A girl like Captain Chubby, maybe, but not Laurie."

Ben didn't argue, he didn't get sore.

"Listen, by the time you get your license, that Mustang will be long gone."

"Long gone where?" Charlie asked.

"Long gone to the dump," Ben answered.

"Maybe that's when I'll finally get my mitts on it," Ack Ack said sorrowfully.

Ben lay on his bed with his Bogie hat tipped over his eye. He rolled a cigarette and sang the Beatles song "You're Gonna Lose That Girl."

He was practically back to normal.

"Laurie's giving me and Arthur a ride to Sammy's," Charlie said. "You want to come?"

"Sweetheart, I think I just might," Ben said. "What is this strange power you have over women?"

Charlie blushed. "She doesn't know how to get there," he said. "I told her I'd show her."

Laurie honked the horn about five minutes later.

"Maybe it'd be easier if you drove," she said to Ben. "I'm not too good at following directions in traffic."

Ben wiped his hands down the sides of his Army surplus pants. "If you insist," he said.

"Beautiful," he kept saying all the way to Sammy's. "Beautiful."

And it was. As they stopped at the red light just before the turn-off for Sammy's, they passed Ack Ack standing on the corner. His bike was in the shop for repairs again.

It was perfect.

Arthur, Charlie, and Ben all leaned out the window and yelled, waving their arms.

Ack Ack was immobilized, glued to the pavement. He rubbed his eyes as if he did not believe what he saw.

The light changed.

"Hey!" Ack Ack started to run alongside. "Where you going?"

"To Sammy's. Follow us!"

Ack Ack made good time. He pulled up huffing and puffing outside Sammy's at the same time the Mustang did.

"How about that?" he said over and over, looking at all of them. "If that isn't something!"

"I almost didn't recognize you without your mustache," Laurie said.

"Yeah." Ack Ack stroked his upper lip. "I feel kind of nude without it."

Sammy flung the door open. "Do my eyes deceive me?" he asked. "Is it my friends, Ben, Charlie, Arthur, Mr. Ackerman?"

Sammy always called Ack Ack Mr. Ackerman.

"I do not believe I know this young lady," Sammy said, his face practically splitting open with his smile.

"This is your lady friend, Ben? I am pleased to make your acquaintance."

"This is just a girl I know," Ben said, embarrassed. "Laurie, this is Sammy."

Laurie and Sammy shook hands.

"A very snappy hat you have on," Sammy said to her. She had on the purple hat with the yellow flowers. "If you should ever want to get rid of it, I would be happy to take it off your hands for a good price."

They all went inside.

"Sit down, sit down," Sammy kept saying. It was as if no time had passed since they had been there last. The tomcat lay on the pattern of sun on the floor and didn't even open his eyes. A train rumbled past and shook the wooden skis and the old golf clubs.

"What's new, Sammy?" Ben asked.

"Nothing much. I still got your items in the back. You never came back for your deposit and I was reluctant to sell the garments until I knew if you wanted them." Sammy's eyes looked very earnest.

"I do if you can wait a little while for the rest of the dough," Ben said. "I am temporarily out of funds."

"Sure," Sammy said happily. "I can wait. I got nothing but time. Anyways, I like having that tail coat and top hat around. Gives the joint a little class. I would not let them go to just anyone. How's the poetry coming?" he asked Arthur, who turned several shades of red, shuffled his feet, and tugged at his ear.

"I got a couple things I would like to ask your opinion on," he said to Sammy.

"Any time, any time at all. Would you be interested in a raccoon coat?" he asked Laurie. "It is not in first-class condition, but it is also not on its last legs. Did you ever see a raccoon coat on its last legs?" Sammy asked and they all laughed.

Laurie tried on the coat.

"Not a bad fit," Sammy said, circling her. "At five bucks, it is not a bad buy."

"If I can pay you tomorrow," Laurie said. "I like it. It would be just the thing for skiing."

"Tomorrow, or the next day. If you are a friend of Ben's, I know you are good for the five bucks," Sammy said. "How about a cup of tea? I am out of saltines but I might scare up a graham cracker or two."

"Next week is my birthday," Sammy said suddenly as they sat sipping the tea. "I am going to be fifty years old." He smiled around the circle.

"A half century. Life begins at fifty, I have decided. They tell you forty, but I say fifty. It is a long time to have been around, that is all I know."

No one said anything. There didn't seem to be anything to say.

The tomcat woke up and surveyed them all. Then he made noises and rubbed himself against Sammy's legs.

"I know you're hungry," Sammy said. "Be patient. I have guests."

"Thanks a lot," Laurie said as they got up to go. "I enjoyed meeting you and I will be back tomorrow with the money."

Sammy nodded. "I look forward to your visit. And don't forget what I said about the hat. Any time you want to get rid of it, I will give you a fair price."

Outside, Ack Ack said to Laurie, "You want me to drive you home?"

"Thanks," she said, "but I have my own car."

"I know," he answered sadly. "That's what I meant. You want me to drive you home in your car?"

"Oh," she said. "Well, all right, I guess. You kids want a ride?"

"It makes me nervous when there are too many people in the car," Ack Ack said.

"Listen, it's hairy enough driving with you when you're cool as a cucumber," Ben said. "We'll play it safe and walk."

Looking nervous herself, Laurie got in the passenger side as Ack Ack slipped behind the wheel.

"If I die tomorrow," he said, "at least I will have had this moment."

"My gosh," Laurie said, "don't say things like that."

"It's just a line from a Ronald Colman movie I happened to catch on the late late show last week," Ack Ack said reassuringly.

As they pulled away from the curb Ben shouted, "Don't forget those seat belts!"

Charlie yelled, "You are carrying precious cargo!" And Arthur chimed in, "Watch out for the fuzz!"

ow'd you make out with Laurie when you drove her home yesterday?" Ben asked Ack Ack.

Charlie hid behind his muffler and eavesdropped.

"I didn't," Ack Ack said. "Make out, that is."

"I didn't mean make out that way and you know it," Ben said. "I mean how'd you do with the car?"

"It was like driving a Rolls," Ack Ack said dreamily. "I must admit, I went a couple miles out of the way just to get maximum out of the buggy. And I saw a whole bunch of kids I know so of course I had to lean on the horn a little just to clear the streets. It was beautiful."

He closed his eyes and smiled. Then he opened them and said, "I fear, however, that it is you she pines for. She's always asking about you, like who do you go out with, are you the type who gets serious right away, stuff like that. Every time I try to bring the conversation around to me, she switches it to you. It is very discouraging." Ack Ack started to stroke his mustache, then he remembered it was gone.

"I think she is pretty nice," Charlie said. "Even if she didn't have her own car. She really talks to you."

"Hey, Charl, I thought you hated girls," Ack Ack said, teasing. "So now all of a sudden you got an eye for the chicks."

"I do not," Charlie protested, blushing. "I just like Laurie. She's not like a girl, anyway, she's more like a boy."

"I'm not sure she'd like to hear that," Ben said.

"Did you happen to get around to the dutch-treat system and find out where she stood on that?" Ack Ack asked.

"No," Charlie said. "But she's very big on women's lib."

"Right on," Ack Ack agreed.

"I have come to a decision," Ben said suddenly, "and it's that I'm not getting involved with any more females. I am going to play the field from now on."

Ack Ack nodded. "More power to you," he said. "And if you can introduce the subject of dutch treat and make it work, you will have struck a blow for men's liberation."

"When the going gets tough, the tough get going," Ben said. "That's what my soccer coach says."

He donned his Bogie hat and a jacket he had recently

bought at Sammy's. "I feel like a new man," he said, putting his hands in the pockets.

"Would you believe?" he asked, an expression of wonder on his face. He drew forth a crumpled bill from the pocket.

"I knew this was my lucky hat!" he marveled. "All I do is put it on and I find a buck. I only paid fifty cents for the darn jacket."

"It could only happen to you," Ack Ack said. "It wouldn't happen to me in a thousand years."

"And I've reached another decision," Ben said. "This is my day for decisions. You know what I'm going to do? I'm going to pay Sammy what I owe him for the tail coat and top hat, take them home, wrap them up, and give them to him for a birthday present. What do you think of that?"

"He'll go out of his mind," Charlie said.

"He'll flip," Ack Ack agreed. "A magnanimous and mature decision. It takes a man to give up something he wants to please another." A puzzled expression crossed his face. "I can't remember what movie that was from," he said.

Ack Ack was lying with his feet propped up on the wall of Ben's bedroom. The feet were pretty dirty due to the fact that Ack Ack went barefoot now that spring was here. Charlie imagined his mother walking in and finding footprints on the wall she had painted so carefully a couple of weeks ago. He smiled, just thinking about it.

"One other thing I thought of," Ben said.

"What's that?"

"If I need it, I can always borrow it—the coat, I mean," Ben said. "I know Sammy would lend it to me."

"Thinking every minute," Ack Ack said, tapping his head.

The telephone rang.

"Oh, hi, Laurie," Charlie said.

"I'm out of here." Ben turned the collar of his jacket up. "I'm gone."

"Hey, Laurie," Ack Ack took the receiver, turning his head from side to side to make sure the coast was clear, "will I do?"

Charlie! The garbage!"

Holy creep, not again!

Charlie wrapped his muffler snugly about his neck and put his hat on. Still no pipe but Sammy had promised he'd keep his eye peeled for a good second- or third-hand one.

"And also," Sammy had said, "should I come across one of them coats with the little cape attached, like the very one Mr. Holmes used to sport, I will pick it up for you. I do not hold out too much hope, as they are not in abundant supply, but I can only say I will try."

Too much. The whole outfit would be too much. Whistling, Charlie went to do his job.

"I want Mary back." Kathy nailed Charlie as he took the lid off the garbage pail. She must've been lying in wait for him. Sticking out her stomach and looking pretty mean and ugly, Kathy whined, "I miss her."

In a pig's eye, Charlie thought to himself. But he had matured and had learned the value of not always voicing one's thoughts aloud.

"Listen," he said in a phony voice a lot like Penny's, "I don't have her any more. I gave her to a little girl who doesn't have any dolls at all. She said she would treat Mary like her own child."

"How come she doesn't have any dolls of her own?" Kathy asked.

"Her family is too poor to buy her any," Charlie said, warming up to his story. "They are so poor she has to eat stale bread and mushrooms every day."

"What's that you've got around your neck?" Kathy asked. She had a short attention span.

"It's the longest muffler in the Western Hemisphere," Charlie said. "It's very special. They say it was used by the Boston Strangler," he finished, lowering his voice.

Kathy settled herself on the back steps. "Who's the Boston Strangler?" she wanted to know.

"You never heard of the Boston Strangler?" Charlie popped his eyes out. This was too good to be true. "You fool, you. Listen, he was the most famous strangler of them all."

"What's a strangler?" Kathy asked.

Charlie outdid himself describing the strangler's activities. Kathy's eyes got bigger and bigger and eventually she got up, sort of slid by Charlie, then hotfooted it for her house, looking back at intervals to make sure Charlie wasn't following her.

Charlie smiled. He'd really taken care of her. She wasn't about to come back. And he wasn't about to give Mary up. Just because the voodoo hadn't worked the first time didn't mean it might not work the second try. It was best to keep Mary around, in case Ben changed his mind.

ABOUT THE AUTHOR

Constance C. Greene is a native New Yorker who attended Marymount School and Skidmore College. Before her marriage she worked on the city desk of the Associated Press.

Mrs. Greene is the author of *Leo the Lioness* and *A Girl Called Al,* which was an ALA Notable Book and an Honor Book in *Book World's* Children's Spring Book Festival. She and her husband and their five children live in Norwalk, Connecticut.